Gossip item in the *San Francisco Chronicle*...

EXTRA

RUMORS OF SECRET WEDDING NO JOKE!

...Will the Hawke finally get his wings clipped? Seems so. According to sources close to the ageless rock-'n'-roll icon, Hawke Faraday will indeed wed his decade-long live-in, former model Caro Sloan.

Time? Top secret.

Location? Top secret.

Security measures rival the Pentagon's. Investigative reporters across the nation are already scrambling to scoop each other. The first tenacious news hound to get this plum is destined for journalism stardom....

Dear Reader,

Personal ads. What single woman (and probably man, for that matter) hasn't taken at least a quick glance through them? Unfortunately, a quick glance is generally more than enough. You know what I'm talking about. "Dark-haired Adonis, 55 (Oh, so that dark hair comes out of a bottle, huh? And Adonis? Wasn't he a *young* guy?), seeks Aphrodite, 21-27 (Aphrodite? Or a daughter?), for good times and hot nights (Maybe hot for you, buddy!)." In short, not too much there for the regular people among us. But then, every so often, you hear about someone who found a gem of a guy—or a woman—that way. Sort of like the way things turn out for Pawnee Walker and Ezra Jagger in Alexandra Sellers' *Not Without a Wife!* Gives the rest of us hope, don't you think?

And then there are Cissy Benton and Jack Cochran, the hero and heroine of Connie Flynn's first Yours Truly novel, *Only Couples Need Apply*. They're two reporters after the same story—and forced to share the same bed to get it. Any way *I* can apply for that job?

So that's it for this month, but don't forget to come back again next month for two more fabulous Yours Truly novels all about unexpectedly meeting, dating—and marrying!—Mr. Right.

Yours,

Leslie Wainger
Senior Editor and Editorial Coordinator

Please address questions and book requests to:
Silhouette Reader Service
U.S.: 3010 Walden Ave., P.O. Box 1325, Buffalo, NY 14269
Canadian: P.O. Box 609, Fort Erie, Ont. L2A 5X3

CONNIE FLYNN

Only Couples Need Apply

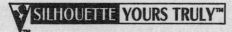

SILHOUETTE YOURS TRULY™

Published by Silhouette Books
America's Publisher of Contemporary Romance

For Kathy Marks, who writes delightful romantic
comedies, reads my work with an eye to the story and
never chides me for the awkwardness of my rocky first
drafts. And for Pat Hebert, who writes in a beautiful
prose I can only envy, intuitively knows what I want
from my characters and steers me right if I go astray.
I lift my cup in thanks.

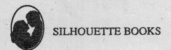 SILHOUETTE BOOKS

ISBN 0-373-52044-1

ONLY COUPLES NEED APPLY

Copyright © 1997 by Constance K. Flynn

About the author

Only Couples Need Apply is my first romantic comedy. Having written longer, more serious stories under the pseudonym of Casey Roberts, I thoroughly enjoyed this chance to cut up. Jack Cochran and Cissy Benton, with their respective ambitions and insecurities, came alive for me. I found myself caught up in their zany antics as they seek love while knowing it will cost one of them a lifelong dream.

Or will it? Maybe it *is* possible to have it all. And because you're reading this, I know you're about to find out.

Writing is…well, an odd life, and at times I struggle to find just the right words to reach your heart. When you enjoy my books you make every hour I spend at the computer worthwhile. So one more time, I'll attempt to enthrall, entertain and amuse you with Jack and Cissy's story. I'll let you be the judge of whether I succeeded.

With warm regards,

Connie Flynn

Prologue

Gossip column item in the *San Francisco Chronicle*...

Will the Hawke finally get his wings clipped?
Seems so. According to sources close to this ageless rock-industry icon, Faraday will indeed wed
his decade-long live-in, former model Caro
Sloan. Time? Top secret. Location? Top secret.
Security measures rival the Pentagon's. Investigative reporters across the nation are already
scrambling to scoop each other. The first tenacious newshound to get this plum is destined for
journalism stardom.

1

Cissy Benton stared out of the San Francisco high-rise window and battled a disgusting bout of self-pity. Excited voices buzzed around her, but Cissy's enthusiasm was as flat as the notes from a sprung guitar string.

She felt an elbow nudge from a tall brunette sitting next to her. "Can you believe it?" the woman whispered into Cissy's ear. "Michael Bolton! I could just die!"

"Wonderful," Cissy replied insincerely. She wanted to be happy for her co-worker, really she did, but...

"Maybe I can talk the Chief into giving you Clint Black," the brunette added sympathetically.

Cissy smiled weakly. "Thanks, but I can take care of myself."

"Sure."

Cissy saw her co-worker's doubtful look and wondered for the umpteenth time why, at nearly thirty years of age, people still viewed her as a defenseless child. Lord knew she'd done her best to dispel the notion. Hadn't she insisted on working her way through college, although her parents could easily afford to pay? Hadn't she honed her writing and photography skills well above industry standards? Hadn't she developed a hard-boiled, prickly demeanor even though it felt unnatural?

Yes! Yes, she had!

So why didn't anyone take her seriously? And this Monday-morning *Top of the Rock* staff meeting was a perfect example. All around her, people were getting important assignments and she was, once again, being overlooked. Reviews. That's what she'd get. All she ever got. Reviews of concerts. Reviews of plays. Reviews of books and movies. Reviews, reviews, reviews.

She hated them.

The magazine's editor in chief cleared his throat, his usual signal that he was about to say something important, and Cissy tore herself away from her dismal thoughts.

"Last, but not least," her boss stated, pausing for dramatic effect, "the Hawke Faraday/Caro Sloan wedding."

The buzzing stopped and all heads snapped in the Chief's direction. Each face at the large conference table wore a look of slavering anticipation.

"The wedding's top secret, so we need someone undercover. That's a real problem. There'll be security all over the place and Hawke and Caro will probably recognize everyone on our staff. Except…"

Cissy's heart skittered, then slowed as she reminded herself it couldn't be true.

"…For Shorty there." The Chief waved his hand in Cissy's direction. Although she hated nicknames referring to her height, that couldn't keep the delighted smile from exploding on her face.

"The kid?" asked an incredulous reporter. Cissy's smile faded.

"She can't handle it alone," protested a junior editor.

"I can help," offered a drop-dead handsome co-worker who'd shown an unreturned romantic interest in Cissy.

Cissy shot to her feet. "I can do this. I'm ready for this story. More than ready."

"Sit down," her boss directed. He surveyed the table and the roar quickly died down. "Our only other option is to hire a stringer, and I'm not trusting this to an outsider. She'll do this piece. Discussion over."

Cissy flopped back down in her chair and let her triumphant smile return. She'd finally been given a second chance. The story of a lifetime and it was hers. All hers. This time she wouldn't blow it.

"Now, here's the deal," her boss advised her. "Soon as we're done, get hold of that friend of yours, the one who runs the domestics agency. See if he can get you a job on Hawke's ranch as a cook or something. If it's humanly possible I'd like to see you up there by nightfall."

Cissy nodded, thinking it unwise to mention that without Hamburger Helper and Tuna Helper she'd be on a starvation diet.

"There's one catch." The Chief tapped a pen thoughtfully on the table as Cissy leaned forward eagerly.

"Yes?"

"Seems Faraday only hires couples. In other words, Shorty, you gotta find yourself a husband."

Across the bay, inside a low, Spanish-style office complex, Jack Cochran hunched under the strong beam of a desk lamp and examined the account books in front of him.

That SOB had taken every dime!

Except for the small emergency fund Jack had stashed away and thankfully forgot to ever mention. Otherwise *Movers & Shakers* would already be history.

Struggling to ignore the gnawing pain of betrayal, Jack penciled down numbers, then ran them through a calculator. When the answer came up, he expelled a breath of relief, but failed to expel the pain.

He'd found his reprieve from inevitable bankruptcy, at least for the next three or four months, but it would take time to get over his shock. Kendall, his partner and best friend—his traitorous best friend, Jack reminded himself—had swept in, swept out, like a thief in the night, and taken everything. His money. His girlfriend. His trust.

Jack grinned bitterly. Sure, they'd been going through inevitable growing pains lately; *Movers & Shakers* was still a fledgling magazine. But it had been their lifelong dream. How could Kendall abandon it like this?

The pencil suddenly splintered in his hands, and he stared down at it, fighting despair. With a frustrated cry, he threw away the pieces and tried to gather his thoughts. He wouldn't give up, *couldn't* give up. There was a way out; he would find it.

A stack of newspapers cluttered a corner of his desk and he picked up the top one, leafing through, searching for a story, *the* story, the one that would send newsstand sales soaring and propel *Movers & Shakers* from gawky adolescence to the full bloom of adulthood.

After scanning several stories, his eyes halted at a small item on the news overview page. He whistled. Had he actually forgotten about Hawke Faraday's upcoming marriage? A private ceremony, time and date undisclosed, place unstated, security very heavy and very visible. Jack's tense features broke into a relieved smile.

The whole world would want to know the tiny little details about that wedding. All Jack needed was a well-connected friend and a suitable alias to find his way around Faraday's security and give the world what it wanted.

He picked up an electronic pocket organizer and punched a button. In milliseconds, he had a name.

JoJo Holloway. Just the man to help him out.

"Can you cook?" Cissy brushed back the blond curls dancing around her face and gave the object of her question a direct brown-eyed stare.

"Huh?" The aging man wore a chauffeur's uniform and he stared at her like he thought she was nuts.

"No, no, darling. Not him!" JoJo Holloway swept across the room, parting a sea of bodies as he moved, and pointed to a man slouching near the door of his plush lobby. "Him!"

Cissy slanted JoJo a doubtful look. The man looked more like one of JoJo's rock-star clients than someone who cooked for them. Unconsciously licking her lips, she quickly scanned the candidate's body. Tall, probably brushing six feet, he wore a leather vest over a blue chambray shirt and jeans that clung to his well-muscled thighs. His long hair, restrained into a sleek ponytail with a leather thong that ended in silver doo-dads, gleamed like mahogany in the light from JoJo's tenth-story windows.

His wide, full mouth looked ready to belt out a rafter-shaking rock tune or kiss the swanlike neck of one of those sleek model types that made Cissy squirm with envy, and that square-chinned, angular face was the antithesis of the all-American type she preferred.

Overall, his image was a shade too dangerous for Cissy's tastes. Not that she wasn't occasionally drawn to such men. Who wouldn't be? Sometimes...

She shook the thought away and found herself staring into a pair of vivid green eyes. The man's mouth turned up, softening the hard angles of his face.

He winked.

With a brief scowl, Cissy returned her attention to JoJo and shook her head. "Nope."

"But he's such a hunk, darling. And he cooks as good as he looks."

"I don't think so, JoJo. I'm looking for someone more..."

Nerdy came to mind. Someone nice and quiet

and—all right she'd better admit it—safe. Someone who would do as he was told. Someone utterly un-appealing and lacking inquisitiveness. This man, well, he didn't fit the bill.

JoJo paid no attention. He gripped Cissy's arm and tugged her forward before she could protest. Again the sea of bodies parted and in a flash she was stand-ing before the man.

"Cissy Benton, meet Jack Cook," JoJo said.

"My pleasure." Jack's husky voice carried the same hint of danger as his appearance, and made Cissy start gazing longingly toward some less ap-pealing male applicants.

"Cissy..." JoJo's warning tone told her he'd no-ticed her wandering attention.

"Right," she said hastily. "Right. Jack the cook."

"No, darling, Jack *Cook*."

"Oh! Jack Cook! Who...cooks?" She giggled somewhat inanely and offered her hand. "Anyone ever tell you you're name's a pun?"

"Many times." He smiled lazily and gave her hand a firm shake. The sheer masculinity of it had Cissy turning away, searching the room for someone closer to her specifications.

"Come along you two," said JoJo, sounding mildly exasperated. "We'll talk in my office."

"But JoJo..."

JoJo hushed her with a sweep of his expressive hands. "Trust me, Cissy. Don't I always come through?"

Finding no argument, Cissy sighed and followed her friend into his spacious office. Jack followed behind her and, as she started to wedge her way between a cluster of outrageously overstuffed chairs, he deftly moved one out of her way.

"Thanks," she said stiffly as she sat down, "but that wasn't necessary. I can take care of myself."

Jack smiled, lines fanning out from the corners of his eyes. "The chair looked too heavy for you to move."

"What do you bet I would've surprised you?" She forced her mouth up, trying to squelch the surge of irritation she always felt whenever people insisted on helping her.

"I'm not a betting man," Jack answered dryly, taking his seat and looking at JoJo.

Cissy felt annoyingly dismissed, but before she could respond, JoJo began talking. "The job's only for this summer. Extra help is needed to serve the guests expected for the wedding." Turning to Cissy, he added. "I'm sure Faraday will think a lady wrangler is *très* sexy."

"Will he feel the same way about a male cook?" Jack asked.

"I don't know, but I bet Caro will be thrilled to her manicured toenails."

JoJo laughed heartily, and Cissy began impatiently tapping her foot. They were only going through these steps to keep Jack from knowing her real reason for taking this job from JoJo. Why did JoJo have to get carried away?

Jack laughed too, although not quite as heartily, then turned toward Cissy. "How long have you been handling horses, Tinker Bell?"

"My name is *Cissy*," she responded through clenched teeth, looking firmly into his eyes. She forgot what she had wanted to say next. Sparkling with laughter, deep pools of glittering emerald green, swirling with dancing lights, his eyes drew her in....

The quizzical flash crossing Jack's face convinced her he was dangerously observant, but she ignored it and launched into her riding history. "I've worked with horses since I was a kid. My five older brothers and sisters worked me like the dickens, but we all ended up having champions. My folks still have my ribbons." She leaned toward him in challenge. "Would you like me to produce them? Would that make you feel better?"

"Cissy has this thing about her height," JoJo explained when Jack shot him a questioning glance. "It might be a good idea not to call her Tinker Bell, or anything else that implies she's short."

"But you *are* short." He turned to Cissy. "What's wrong with that?"

Little he knew, Cissy thought, giving the length of him a clearly resentful once-over. He had never needed to stand on a chair to get something off the top of a refrigerator, had never received a condescending pat on the top of that gorgeous head of his. She was about to say just that, when he spoke again.

"It's hard to imagine a little thing like you pushing around a great big horse."

Cissy shot up to her full five feet. That did it! "You don't have to be big to handle horses, Jack," she said, imitating the scalding tone her father used every time she disappointed him. "Just smarter than they are."

She couldn't remember a time she hadn't been treated like a fluff ball. This story was her big chance to show the world there was more to her than met the eye, but she could get it without enduring the same kind of treatment. She turned to face JoJo, to ask him to end the meeting. Jack Cook wouldn't do.

No, he wouldn't do at all.

2

"**S**marter than horses?" While Jack knew his ex-
girlfriend Michelle didn't represent the entire female
population, his current antagonism toward women in
general spilled onto Cissy. "I can only hope you
are."

When Cissy let out an annoyed sound and wriggled
on the ridiculously large chair, trying to lever herself
out, Jack leaned forward. He was out of here!

This wouldn't work. Cissy made him think of the
cheerleader who'd dumped him in the eighth grade.
She was cute as...what? A kitten? A button? Who
knew? But she definitely wasn't sugar and honey.
More like pepper, which he'd never been particularly
fond of.

Even if she weren't so peppery, he'd have reser-
vations. He'd asked JoJo for an introverted horsey
type. Someone who would keep to herself while he
did his work. This blond-haired woman-child clearly
didn't qualify. She'd tag along, ask questions, maybe
even learn his real name. Before he knew it, his cover
would be blown.

"Uh, JoJo, could we talk a minute?" he said.
"Outside."

"Go ahead, JoJo." Cissy folded her arms across her chest. "When you get back, let's talk about finding me the nerd I requested."

That was the first thing Jack heard her say in his favor. Although she clearly thought he qualified for jerkdom, she apparently didn't consider him a nerd. What remained unclear was the reason for her hostility. Judas Priest, all he'd done was call her Tinker Bell. He'd heard of men having height complexes. But a woman?

JoJo didn't budge, and after nearly a minute elapsed Jack looked at him expectantly, noticing Cissy do the same.

"Sorry, darlings. The combinations you two requested are in short supply. What you see is what you get."

Jack and Cissy groaned in tandem. After a heavy pause, their eyes met.

"So what do you think?" Only his love for his magazine made Jack ask the question.

Cissy tapped her foot. "I guess there's no choice."

JoJo grinned and picked up the phone. "Okay, darlings," he said after hanging up. "Start packing. As of now, the newlywed Mr. and Mrs. Jack Coch—, er, Cook, are employed at the Rockin' Hawke Ranch. A limo will be here at two o'clock to drive you to Reno. Don't be late.

"After you pack, there's one thing left to do." JoJo paused, laid a finger beside his nose, seeming to relish what he was about to say next. "Shop for wedding rings. Something suitably expensive."

Jack saw Cissy look down wistfully at her bare

finger, and as JoJo went on to explain that he'd set up a deal with a jeweler friend to rent rings for such "uh, contingencies," he wondered what was going through her blond head. Was she warring with some nearly forgotten dream that didn't include bedecking that finger until she'd wed her lifetime mate?

Well, she'd have to handle that on her own. He owed her a little tit for tat. He'd buy Cissy a ring so big and gaudy, she wouldn't be able to lift her hand.

It was all he could do not to chuckle out loud. Revenge was sweet.

"Are you having a big wedding?" asked the jewelry clerk as she placed a velvet-lined ring tray on the glass counter.

"Uh...well..." After dashing home, hurriedly packing, then dragging her luggage back to JoJo's, Cissy had barely arrived at the jewelry store on time. Still feeling rushed, she hadn't anticipated such a question. She glanced over at Jack for help. He smiled wickedly and said nothing.

Tapping her foot in agitation, she gave him a small nudge, but he remained infuriatingly silent. After an awkward pause, Cissy finally answered the woman. "A small, private wedding, we think. Right, honey?"

"Right." He patted his back pocket. "We're trying to keep it easy on the wallet."

He placed an affectionate arm on Cissy's shoulders. Nothing too personal, she noticed, just warm and friendly, probably meant to impress the clerk. But her feelings toward this man were anything but warm.

Hostile and jumbled maybe, but not warm and friendly. She discreetly shrugged his arm away.

Ignoring the rebuff, Jack touched a bridal set dripping with diamonds. "If I know my sweetie, she'll break the bank by choosing this one."

Cissy suppressed a choking sound. The clerk smiled approvingly, as she asked if the ring would suit.

"Oh no, it's much too expensive." She certainly didn't want to say it looked like it came from a gum ball machine.

Jack grinned impishly. "Nothing's too good for my Tinker Bell." He lifted the ring from its slot. "Here, sweetie, try it on."

"You can't be serious, Jack." Dear God, it was ugly. Surely Jack wasn't planning to force it on her.

Surely he was. He picked up her hand with his long, tanned fingers and put on the ring. "Marvelous," he crooned. "We'll take it."

"Wonderful!" The clerk beamed as she took out her sales book. Cissy knew the woman wasn't privy to the store's arrangement with JoJo and was probably working up her commission on some internal cash register. Well, Cissy hated to disappoint, but...

"No, Jack," she protested. "We can't." She began slipping the ring off. "Really!"

He cupped her hands between his and stared in her eyes with mock devotion. "Like I said, nothing's too good for my sweetie." Then, slanting a glance at the clerk, he directed her to wrap it up.

The woman bustled off to find a box.

"I don't like the ring, Jack."

"It's a done deal." He dismissed her objection with an idle movement of his hand, then looked away.

Cissy inspected the bauble on her hand sadly. She'd heard something plaintive in her protest, wondered if Jack heard it, too. She reminded herself it didn't matter—it was all a sham, a make-believe ring, a make-believe marriage. Still, something felt all wrong.

She'd never chosen a diamond before. Although she'd once been briefly engaged, in the end she'd realized she hadn't loved the domineering Ed enough to commit to him for a lifetime. The sacrifices he'd asked were greater than she could give.

Since then, she'd expended most of her energy on her career, giving little thought to marriage, weddings and rings. Not until this disturbingly genuine shopping trip had she revisited any of her girlhood dreams.

Somehow this stranger beside her was weaving himself into those forgotten memories, and foisting the ugliest ring in history on her. It seemed so unfair.

As Jack followed Cissy's dismayed gaze down to the tasteless bridal set, he was shamelessly pleased with himself. He knew she hated it, that it would embarrass her, and felt his revenge was exquisitely complete.

But as he stared at the flash of overdone diamonds, it occurred to him that Kendall would probably buy such a set for Michelle. She'd drool over it, display it proudly to all her friends and never realize the vulgarity that was so apparent to Cissy.

Jack suddenly liked Cissy better for having the

good taste to hate the ring. But why wasn't she battling for a different set? How unlike her.

Had she caught on?

Of course she had! And was probably determined not to give him any pleasure in his little triumph. Now *that* was like her.

He lifted **his** gaze and looked into Cissy's eyes, which had made him think of luscious, shiny Hershey's Kisses when they'd first met. Now they seemed to be melting, echoing the faint ache in her voice he had ignored at the time. Suddenly pulled into the depths of those round, sad pools he felt a tug at his heart, soft, yet releasing an aching melody. It sang of the vulnerability beneath Cissy's brittle shell and behind his own shield of sarcasm. His amusement vanished. Wanting to shatter the mood, he forced a cough. It didn't work.

The clerk returned, waving a box.

"We've changed our minds," Jack pointed at a delicate marquise solitaire with subtle scrolls on its gold setting. "We'll take that one."

Cissy's face lit up and he knew he'd made the perfect choice.

But when she tried the rings on, looking slightly awestruck, the song in his heart turned unbearably sweet. Seeking a way to escape its intensity, he said, "Maybe it will turn you into the perfect wife, Tinker Bell. Lord knows you need the help."

Cissy stood on the curb in front of JoJo's office building, nervously twisting the bands on her third finger, left hand. The set's diamond baguettes melded seamlessly with the dainty solitaire and it *was* exquisite. Somehow Jack had unerringly anticipated her preference, which only made her feel worse. This was the kind of ring she'd imagined accepting from the man she would eventually marry. Not, as was the case, bestowed by some sarcastic and insulting partner in crime.

She wanted to deny it, but his last remark had stung, and as he dropped her luggage down beside her, she gave him a resentful glance.

"Did you pack your entire closet?" he asked, making a big show of the exhaustion she knew he didn't feel.

She normally insisted on carrying her own bags, but she'd wanted to punish Jack for his nasty comment. Succumbing to that wicked urge, she'd swept out of JoJo's office, blithely ordering Jack to bring the luggage.

Unfortunately, Jack didn't seem to view it as punishment even though it had taken two trips. He seemed inordinately pleased at providing this little service. After lining her bags near the curb, he arranged his own hard-sided luggage into a makeshift bench. "Let's make ourselves comfortable till the driver gets here." As Cissy moved toward the suitcases, he pointed at the leather case slung over her shoulder. "Here, let me take that one, too."

"No!" Cissy placed her hand protectively over the strap. "My boss would—"

She clamped her lips shut, already searching for a response to Jack's inevitable question.

"Boss?" Jack frowned quizzically.

"Yeah, well, that is, this case means a lot to me." She patted it with exaggerated fondness. "That's it, yes. It was a going-away gift from my previous boss. I'd die if I lost it. Sentimental value, that kind of thing...."

Jack shrugged, then sank to the suitcases and patted the empty space beside him. "There's room for you, too."

Cissy considered refusing, but could find no good reason for it, so she smoothed the slacks of her yellow linen pantsuit and sat next to him. The space was tight and his knee brushed her thigh. She scooted away.

"An accident." He smiled knowingly.

"Hmm." Propping her elbows on her knees, she rested her head on her hands and stared forward. A breeze, unusually warm for a May afternoon in San Francisco, swept paper and leaves down the gutter. The bustling Monday traffic rolled by, tires slapped the pavement. In spite of the background hum, Cissy could hear Jack's breath.

No, not exactly *hear,* she could *feel* it, almost as if it were her breath, her chest, moving in, moving out. A disorienting sensation. Inexplicably, it reminded her of the subject she knew must eventually be dealt with.

"Let's reach an agreement about sleeping arrangements." She stared forward stiffly. "There'll probably be only one bedroom, so we can trade off. You sleep in the living room one night, I'll sleep there the next night."

"You think we'll have a spacious suite up there?"

"Of course. Faraday has money to burn."

"I doubt he spends it on the hired help. We'll be lucky to get a queen-size bed."

"Oh, Jack." Cissy gave him a scornful look. "Don't you know anything? These people live larger than life—so does their staff."

Jack's laugh made her feel foolish. "Admit it, Jack," she challenged. "You don't know anything about it!"

"Maybe not. But don't be surprised if I'm right." He'd been looking over her shoulder as he spoke, and he now stood up. "We'll find out soon enough. Here's the limo."

Cissy rose also. Jack picked up his bags and began moving them to the curb.

"The driver will get them," Cissy said.

"He's our co-worker, not our servant," Jack chided. "We're not going on a fancy vacation."

No question about that, Cissy thought.

The limousine pulled to the curb and a liveried black man with a bearlike physique stepped out and opened the trunk. Jack began passing luggage to him.

Over Jack's protests, Cissy pitched in with the loading, her misgivings growing with every bag she handed over. She had no idea how long she'd have to stay at the Faraday ranch. The wedding could be as late as September. How would she handle Jack all that time? It irked her to realize that she'd given up her first big reporting opportunity for a man, and now here was another man—one who meant nothing to her—jeopardizing her second one.

He was definitely a hazard. In a few short hours, he'd proven he'd forever be in her face. Worse, look what she'd blurted out when he'd tried to take her shoulder bag. This was only the first day. What if she slipped up again?

She bent to get in the car, glancing wistfully at JoJo's tenth-story office, longing to go back and find a different, less intrusive partner. As she was telling herself it was already too late, the swat landed on her rear.

"Jack!" She whirled, almost smacking her head against the top of the door. "What are you *doing?*"

"Getting into my role as your lusty new husband."

"Not in public, darling." Painfully aware that the driver was holding the door, Cissy gave him a frozen smile.

"Newlyweds," the man commented, amused.

Cissy kept the smile in place until she and Jack got seated, and the driver had settled in the glassed-off driving compartment. Then she turned on him with fury.

"Don't ever, ever do that again!"

He tried to look contrite, but his devilish smile told her differently.

Cissy sighed in futility. "Why are you always tormenting me, Jack?"

"Was that torment?" His green eyes widened innocently. "Can't a man pat his wife on the fanny?"

"I'm not your wife! Don't even begin acting like I am!"

"Okay, Cissy, I'll back off." He laughed softly, clearly feeling like he'd won this skirmish. "But one thing. When we get to the ranch, if there's only a single bed, we're bunking together."

"In your dreams, Jack. In your dreams."

3

Cissy plunked her carryall on the end of the chenille-covered double bed, dismayed. Their cabana had only that single lumpy-looking bed, a battered chest of drawers, two torn and faded armchairs and one scarred end table. A couple of cheap rugs were scattered about the worn asphalt flooring. So much for the lavish life-style of those who served the rich and famous, she thought, even more dismayed because Jack had been right.

She backed up, hoping to discover an overlooked door leading to a second room, and ran into a warm-blooded obstacle.

Jack!

His scent—cypress and juniper and something deliciously smoky—rode on her intaken breath. When his large hands gripped her shoulders, she jumped.

"Whoa," he exclaimed.

"Why did you creep up on me like that?" She turned, pulling from his grasp. Big mistake. Now she was all but plastered to his leather-and-denim-covered chest.

"I didn't exactly have a choice." He inched back into the open doorway to give her room.

Good grief! The room was so small, she'd be bumping into him every time she turned around. She retreated and hit the end of the bed. Her heavy shoulder bag, still securely in place, swung back, causing her balance to waver. Deciding not to fight it, she plopped down.

"At least there's some floor space over here." She pointed to a spot between the bed and the bathroom entrance that was little more than three feet wide, then tilted her head to look up at Jack. "You can put your bedroll there."

Jack dropped his bags. One came so close, she felt a rush of air against her leg. "Did you forget what I told you in the limo?" he said in a patient-if-it-kills-me tone.

"I put it out of my mind."

"Well, let it back in. Or is there only room for one thought at a time in there?"

Cissy blew at a strand of hair that had fallen over her eyes. "Look, the driver's waiting outside and I need to get my suitcases."

"I'll help you," he offered. "We can talk on the way."

Cissy knew the gesture was an offhanded apology and her exasperation faded. But she had deliberately left the suitcases behind so she could interview the driver on the sly, and Jack would just be in the way.

She shook her head. "I can handle it."

"Whatever." Still standing in the doorway, Jack swung his suitcase on top of the dresser.

Cissy got up and found herself staring at the decorations hanging from Jack's ponytail thong. They were three-dimensional eagles, beautifully fashioned out of solid silver, and she fought an urge to pick up one of them and run her fingers over its sleek surface.

"Excuse me." She gave Jack a gentle shove. He pressed against the wall, making room for her to climb over his remaining suitcase. As she went through the door, he grumbled, "I'm not sleeping on the floor. Count on it."

Cissy cursed in frustration, punctuating it by slamming the door. Glaring ineffectually at the blank door, Jack twisted the gold band on his left hand.

It already chafed. Undoubtedly, Cissy's rings were chafing too. He couldn't honestly blame her, what with the way his mouth so often ran away with him. Not that Cissy was any sweet-talking angel herself. Yet, facts were facts. She was going to be his partner for several weeks to come. There had to be some way to make peace.

Obviously, he wasn't very good at choosing partners, otherwise he wouldn't be sitting in this tiny room, stuck for weeks with this pepper pot while Kendall enjoyed both Michelle's companionship and the profits from the magazine.

He still felt raw from the loss. In moments of brutal self-honesty, he realized he and Michelle had been barreling toward a breakup anyway, and nothing she might have done would have surprised him. But Kendall... That was a different story. His betrayal shattered a lifetime of trust. It made Jack doubt himself, doubt his instincts. At least about people.

But not for hot stories. He trusted that instinct completely, and knew the Faraday wedding was hotter than blazes, guaranteed to keep the doors of *Movers & Shakers* open.

Memories—once fond, now agonizing—suddenly filled Jack's mind. His thoughts went back to the day the dream had been born. He and Kendall were coeditors, reporters and whatever-the-hell-had-to-be-done-doers for *Knight Beat,* their high school newspaper. Paul McCartney was in concert in the Bay Area and someone dared them to get pictures.

Accepting the challenge, they sneaked backstage. All too soon a pair of burly security guards booted them out, but they laughed victoriously as the stage door slammed in their faces.

They'd already snapped the pictures! What heroes they'd been when that paper came out. They spent the day receiving congratulatory backslaps and the night conceiving *Movers & Shakers,* vowing never to quit until they succeeded.

But Kendall *had* quit, nearly ripping the dream from Jack's hand. Now it was his alone, and at nearly thirty-five he'd be damned if he'd give up without a fight! Bankruptcy wasn't the end of the world, he supposed, but he wouldn't go down easily, if only to prove that he didn't need Kendall any more than Kendall needed him. And being inconvenienced by snippy Cissy Benton was a small price to pay.

Jack unlatched his suitcase and began putting away his meticulously folded clothing. He staked his claim on the top drawers, defending his ungentlemanly actions with assurances that Cissy wouldn't have to bend as far to open the bottom ones.

Where was she anyway? She'd left over ten minutes ago. Surely a woman who tamed wild horses could fetch her suitcases in less time than that. On the other hand, why should he care?

But he did. And that annoyed the hell out of him. From the minute he'd laid eyes on her in JoJo's office, she'd stirred his protective instincts, like some defenseless kid sister. How could anyone be that small? He could probably span her shapely waist with his hands and have room left over. Plus, he'd always been a sucker for curly blond hair. A brown-eyed blond was nearly irresistible.

Who was he kidding? He didn't have a kid sister, just a couple of rowdy younger brothers he'd watched over all their lives. His feelings for Cissy were anything but fraternal and could become a major distraction. His mind wandered in ways totally inconsistent with brotherly impulses and he yanked them back, deciding he'd better sleep on the floor after all. Cissy could stay out there with the driver forever as far as he was concerned. But...

Weren't they supposed to be at the main house for a briefing? Jack glanced at his watch. Yeah, in less than an hour, and they still had to change their clothes.

Deciding to give her another ten minutes, he patted his underwear into geometric piles, then slid the drawer shut. Duffel bag in hand, he went to the bathroom medicine cabinet, grimaced into its cracked mirror, then lined up his shaving supplies by size, barely aware that he'd left the bottom shelves for his shorter-than-short roommate.

He glanced at his watch again. Time was up. He wasn't about to let her jeopardize his story on the first day. Working up a steamful of righteous indignation, he stalked out of the cabana and headed out. As he neared the road, he heard voices.

"Doesn't anyone know where the wedding will be held?" Cissy was asking the chauffeur.

"Only Mr. Jordon." The driver leaned against the limousine, touching the hood possessively. "We're expecting him any day so he can finish the arrangements."

"Is that so?"

"True fact."

Jack stepped behind a concealing bush, his indignation vanishing, and reached inside his leather vest to turn on a microrecorder.

"I hate to admit it, Saul," Cissy said. "But I don't know who Jordon is."

"No?" Saul didn't seem surprised. "He's Mr. Hawke's business manager. He kinda keeps low, so most folks don't know that."

"Hmm," Cissy purred, nodded. Then she changed the subject. "Caro is so gorgeous. I'll bet her wedding gown will be absolutely stunning."

"I don't know much about it, myself, but the missus does. She's Miss Caro's personal maid, and they're shopping for a gown in Barcelona right now."

"Oh, wow! You think she'd tell me about it?"

The black man hesitated, touched his chin. "Well, um, don't mean to sound snooty, but me and Mama don't usually socialize with, um, seasonal help. Miz Katchum—you'll meet her tonight—she kinda frowns on it." Then he smiled broadly. "But Mama's been wanting horse riding lessons, and the regular wranglers kinda give her a hard time. I think she'll want to meet you. Let me ask."

Cissy muttered something about understanding and being happy to teach Mama, but sounded disappointed. Jack, however, squashed an urge to cheer. Without realizing it, Cissy was a natural-born interviewer, and it looked like she was getting them in with the permanent staff. As her "husband," he'd have every right to tag along with his trusty recorder deep in his pocket.

Saul moved to pick up one of Cissy's overstuffed garment bags. "Here, let me take in this here luggage for you, seeing how your husband just traipsed right off."

"Oh, thanks," Cissy squealed appreciatively. It sounded forced to Jack, as though she were putting on an act, but he dismissed it as a reaction to their stressful day. Having heard enough, he stepped out from the brush.

"Cissy, honey," he called cheerfully.

"Oh. Jack. Hi." She looked displeased.

He stuck out a friendly hand to Saul as he approached. "Thanks for offering, pal, but my little lady here is very independent."

"So I noticed." The man gave Jack a firm handshake. "We didn't do introductions earlier. The name's Saul Coolidge."

Jack gave his name and released Saul's hand. He

then assumed control of Cissy's luggage and draped an affectionate arm over her shoulder. "Cissy and I have to hurry along or we'll be late for the meeting. She has this tendency to dawdle." He chucked her chin with his free hand. "Don't you, sweetie?"

He took the garment bag from Saul, then pointed to Cissy's wheeled suitcase. "Get that, will you?"

Cissy looked bemused as he whisked her and the luggage up the path, but Jack heard a growl in her voice when she said, "You do that again, you'll be putting your manhood at risk."

"Do what?" These spats were becoming a regular thing.

"Manhandle me."

Jack tried to bite his tongue and failed. "Baby, if you think that's manhandling, you ain't seen nothing yet."

Cissy stopped dead in her tracks, looked back to see that Saul had driven away. Then, head tilted defiantly, she went chin to collarbone with him. "I've had all I'm going to take from you, mister. Let's get something straight. We need each other for these jobs, but that's *all* I need or want from you. So, hands off!"

Jack lifted both arms in the air and forced a grin. "No hands, see?"

Her eyes narrowed and she tossed her head. "Do you care about anything, Jack? Or is it all a joke to you?"

She almost sounded like she really wanted to know, and for a heartbeat Jack wanted to tell her everything. About Kendall, about Michelle, about how much he cared about *Movers & Shakers*. How it was the only thing he cared for anymore.

He let out a breath, waiting for the impulse to pass.

"Well?" she implored.

"Life's easier if you blow a lot of it off, Cissy. Something you might want to consider." Her eyelashes lifted and he hurried before she could interrupt. "Maybe you're right. Hell, you are right. I have been tormenting you a little. But you're not helping. Believe it or not, I have no plans to ravish you. This is a business arrangement for me, too, and it could be a whole lot pleasanter if you'd stop being so defensive."

He expected her to blow up, but she remained quiet, regarding him thoughtfully. He wondered what wheels were spinning behind those luscious eyes.

"Okay," she finally said. "But I still want to make the rules clear."

"I get your message." Jack smiled in relief. "I promise to treat you with respect, if you'll treat me with the same."

"It's not just that." She bit her lips and looked away. "It's...well, you know, we're supposed to be newlyweds. People think... I never thought..." Screwing up her face like she was steeling herself for a doctor's needle, she blurted, "Oh, Jack, I can't go around hugging and kissing you, but everyone will expect it!"

Jack laughed heartily. "Don't worry, Tinker Bell. We'll tell 'em we don't believe in public displays of affection."

"You think that will work?"

Jack nodded, despite some nagging doubts.

She looked like a load had been lifted from her shoulders. Then she frowned. "One more thing."

Jack tilted his head in anticipation.

"Stop calling me Tinker Bell. And stop treating me like a kid." She lifted her chin again. "I may be little, but I can take care of myself!"

"I wasn't…" Of course, he was. He'd questioned her horsemanship, he'd chosen her wedding band, he'd tried to take over loading her luggage. He'd even chosen her dresser drawers and medicine cabinet shelves, and she'd probably be quite unhappy when she discovered that fact.

"Yeah, okay. It's just, well, you're so cu—"

"Don't even say it!" She grinned, but it held a warning.

He returned the grin, and for one quiet second got lost in it. Then, remembering the orientation meeting, he told Cissy they'd better hurry.

As she fell in beside him, she glanced over.

"Now," she said impishly, "about the sleeping arrangements."

4

———➤◆◄———

The Rockin' Hawke Ranch encompassed several thousand acres and was a true working spread. As Cissy and Jack putted the three-quarter-mile distance toward the main house in a small electric cart the ranch had provided, she surveyed the grounds.

Cattle, looking like multicolored pushpins, grazed on distant range grass. A horse whickered somewhere in the barn. She inhaled the mingled scents of clean air and honest dirt and settled back with a satisfied sigh. May was a wonderful time of year to be in the Nevada mountains, and cramped living quarters notwithstanding, this assignment offered many pleasures.

"Nice change from the city, isn't it?" Jack's purring voice echoed her contentment.

"Exactly what I was thinking."

An easy silence fell between them, but as Jack wheeled the cart into a crammed parking lot, he looked Cissy over.

"You sure about that outfit?" He had voiced the same concern back at the cabana.

Cissy smoothed her ecru riding jacket over its matching jodhpurs. "I told you, Jack, I want to look professional."

"Yeah, but, I just think—it's still not too late to go back and change, you know—I just don't think anyone else will dress that way. You might feel uncomfortable."

Cissy made a disbelieving sound. Here they'd been having a pleasant moment and he'd ruined it as usual. "I've lived on ranches all my life, Jack, and have always worn English riding habits. People expect it when you're teaching or taking care of their expensive horses."

"Yeah, but Faraday is different. He's a rock star, and they—"

"Why do you think you know everything? I'll lay odds you're the one who'll feel uncomfortable." She ran her eyes over Jack's attire. He'd put on a pair of jeans and an open-necked cotton shirt over which he'd thrown the leather vest. Except for the colors, he looked much as he had all day.

Jack stopped the cart, turned it off and looked at Cissy. "It's your funeral."

Did he ever give up? Cissy flounced out of the cart and started toward the house without him. He quickly caught up and minutes later they were in a huge great room.

Cissy fought a desire to gape. Dominating one wall was a beehive fireplace that snapped and crackled with a blaze so large she wanted to call the fire department. The flames were mirrored in the floor-to-ceiling windows that overlooked snow-capped mountains and a valley of undulating green. Groups of Southwestern furniture were casually clustered around heavy Navajo rugs.

Everywhere, people—crushed together on the couches, floating across the terra-cotta floor, talking, laughing. The size of Hawke Faraday's staff amazed her. So did their clothing, as she knew Jack would soon point out. The room was a veritable sea of denim, wrinkled cotton and leather.

She stood out like a peacock in a chicken coop. Jack nudged her and grinned knowingly as a mortified blush stained her cheeks. For an instant, she wanted to deck him, but then remembered their afternoon talk when Jack so accurately hit the mark. Her sense of humor *had* gotten lost in her anxiety about the assignment. It wouldn't hurt to lighten up. After all, the world wouldn't end just because she'd overdressed.

Returning Jack's smile, she mouthed, "You were right," which she was certain provided his thrill for the year. Then, determined not to cling to him for moral support, she walked away.

As her composure returned, a willowy woman entered the room. Her soft knit pants and stripped tunic were color coordinated, which made Cissy feel marginally better.

"People, people," the woman called out. "Let's begin."

The din receded. She introduced herself as Bonnie Katchum, Staff Coordinator, then passed out a pamphlet and covered the contents with quick, nervous gestures.

There were very few rules: show up sober for shifts; stay on the grounds when on call; no foodstuff or cooking in the rooms. Buffet-style meals began early and ended late. Apparently, food was a high priority on the Rockin' Hawke, which meant Jack would be kept very busy in the kitchen.

Done with the rules, Bonnie made rounds, taking time to introduce new employees to their supervisors. She presented Cissy to the head wrangler, a Saint-Bernard-size man called Tiny, who told her to report to the barn at seven-thirty the next morning. Although he kept mum about her attire, he eyed the outfit suspiciously.

Cissy noticed Jack talking to a man whom she surmised was the head cook; then she meandered around the room. She was staring at a Remington Western painting, certain it was an original, when everyone began filing outside.

Following suit, she walked out onto a covered patio that stretched to forever and was festooned with countless tiny lights. Dozens of picnic tables, set with silverware and condiment holders, filled the bricked area. As the tangy aroma of barbecue sauce reached her nose, Cissy's stomach growled.

"Hungry?" Jack asked, suddenly appearing at her side.

"Very. A woman could gain weight here."

"Don't be so sure. I have a feeling they'll work the pounds right off you."

"Oh?" From the festive atmosphere, that wasn't the feeling Cissy got, but the next day would tell. She and Jack fell in at the end of the food line, where she had a hard time choosing from the abundant array.

The tables filled up fast and it took a while before Cissy and Jack found seats. They settled in, interrupting a spirited conversation in progress.

"Anyway," continued a young brunette woman after introductions were completed, "I think the wedding's going to be here on the ranch. This is our third summer, and I've never, ever, seen so many employees."

Cissy's ears perked up. Slipping a hand into her waist pack, she clicked on her recorder.

"Nah, no way, Terry," someone countered. "They'll fly out for the big day. The ranch is too obvious."

"That's why it's *perfect!* Don't you see? Nobody would think of it. If I were Hawke and Caro, that's what I'd do. Send everyone chasing after the secret location, then—"

Terry shot upright, eyes agog. "My God, there he is!"

All heads turned to follow her stare.

Hawke Faraday. He stood near a lattice fence, wearing cutoffs and a baggy T-shirt that proclaimed Fly With the Hawke, and surveyed the patio like a king inspecting his domain. His trademark hair sprang up in ragged wheat-colored tufts, and his eyes glittered like the dusky sky behind him. The energy shift on the patio was palpable.

When he stopped to talk to Bonnie Katchum, the diners returned to their meals, taking up conversation again. Cissy noticed that the wedding wasn't mentioned again.

She'd been told that most of her co-workers had worked at the ranch for several seasons, so their reactions surprised her. She thought star-struckness wore off after a while. Apparently not.

A man across from her looked over. "Heard you two are newlyweds."

Cissy, mouth full of food, just nodded. Jack gave a noncommittal "Uh-huh."

"So where'd you get married?"

Cissy swallowed. "Santa Barbara." Her words collided with Jack's simultaneously offered "Las Vegas."

The man's laugh was joined by several others.

"They're already at it," Terry said, a snide edge in her voice. "Can't even agree on where they got married."

"Actually," Jack explained, "Cissy wanted Santa Barbara, but I persuaded her to go to Vegas." Cissy felt his toe nudge hers. "You weren't *too* disappointed, were you, honey?"

"No, no, sweetheart," she replied, grinning wickedly. "Especially after I talked you out of the chapel where the minister was an Elvis impersonator."

That sparked another burst of laughter and Jack smiled, then nudged Cissy harder.

"The important thing was that we did it." He lifted Cissy's ring hand and placed both of their hands on the table. "After all this time, we're now Mr. and Mrs. Jack Cook."

Cissy's hand rested loosely on top of Jack's, her diamond sparkling above his gold band in the magical lights of the patio. It occurred to her that they looked like a couple in a jewelry ad, one of those kind that declared diamonds were forever. She knew Jack expected her to make a show of unity, but she said precisely what popped into her mind the minute Jack lifted her hand.

"He's Mr. Jack Cook. I'm Mrs. Cissy Benton Cook."

"Ah," said one of the men. "You've got yourself a modern woman. Boy, your work's cut out for you."

Cissy and Jack were spared the need to respond when the man's wife leaned over and touched the ring. "It's so beautiful," she cooed. "I always wanted a ring like that."

Cissy pretended to preen, but her foot began tapping, provoking another nudge from Jack. This had been the longest Monday of her life and the pretense was taking more energy than she could spare. When the woman let go of her hand, she relaxed, sure the group's attention would move elsewhere. Then the woman asked, "Do you have plans for children? They're so hard in our line of work."

"I was hoping for a baseball team," Jack said without missing a beat.

"H-he's k-k-kidding." It was Cissy's turn to foot-nudge.

Everyone laughed, then mercifully talk drifted to the other diners' children. The difficulty of finding employers who accepted them, schooling expense. Pretty soon came the subject of braces and doctor bills. Just as the terrible twos arose, a new hush fell over the table. Cissy turned to see Bonnie approaching with Hawke. The man was pointedly staring in her direction.

Her mouth turned dry as sand. Had she been struck dumb by the prospect of meeting a star, or was Hawke

Faraday's lascivious expression the cause? Surely she was imagining the appreciative look in his eyes.

Not.

Hawke shook Jack's hand perfunctorily, but when Cissy extended her hand, he held on and pulled up until she hovered awkwardly between the bench and the table.

"Come on out, honey. Let me get a look at you." His words were friendly, yet clearly a command.

Cissy climbed out from the bench and shot Jack a glance, hoping for a hint on how a wife should act under these circumstances. He responded by putting a clearly possessive hand on her arm.

Hawke's gaze flickered to Jack's hand, then to his face. Their eyes locked in momentary battle. Then, openly dismissing Jack, Hawke returned his attention to Cissy.

"Aren't you the tiniest little thing." He scanned her from head to toe. His gaze lingered on her round breasts. If Jack had treated her this way, Cissy knew she would have taken him out with one lash of her tongue.

Wishing she could unleash it on Hawke, she instead murmured a demure "nice to meet you," and told Hawke she looked forward to working with his horses.

He seemed surprised. "Is this the new wrangler?" he asked Bonnie. When the coordinator nodded, Hawke turned back. "I expected some prune-faced wench." He grimaced, as though the thought was too repulsive to dwell upon. "What a pleasure it is to find an angel instead."

Releasing one of Cissy's hands, he took hold of her chin. Fighting a tremor of distaste, she reflexively twisted her head away, then yanked her remaining hand free.

Hawke smirked knowingly, as if enjoying her resistance.

"There are more people to meet," Bonnie murmured. Hawke nodded and moved on, but not before telling Cissy, "I'll catch up with *you* later."

Shaken and fuming, Cissy climbed back on the bench. Jack's face-splitting grin didn't help any, and when he turned to her and whispered a mocking "*I* can take care of myself," she almost screamed. Here, she'd thought he had been protecting her. Of course his protection was the last thing she wanted, but she'd felt his efforts merited at least a glimmer of gratitude. Wrong.

Pointedly ignoring him, she fell to reassuring herself. Hawke probably came on to all his female employees at first. She'd vanish from his mind before he crossed the patio.

"Oooh, you're so-o-o lucky," Terry said with a pout. "He's never taken that much interest in me."

"He must like tiny little things," Jack said.

Cissy stared at him balefully. Jack roared with laughter, turning heads at the surrounding tables.

Great, Cissy thought. She had a comedian in her bedroom and a rock star who wanted to be there. And although the pouty Terry might not understand it, Cissy would prefer the comedian any day.

5

Jack took great pains to act amused, but Hawke's advances to Cissy had actually bothered him a lot. The guy was a shark, and from what Jack could see, Cissy was too inexperienced to keep him from gobbling her up. But he had to proceed with caution. Cissy would view his efforts on her behalf as interference.

He saw that she was worried, too. She betrayed it with the little lines between her eyebrows, and by the way she nibbled her lower lip when she thought no one was looking. She'd hardly touched her pie after Terry's revealing comment.

When their dinner companions began scattering, she turned to him, looking drained and at wit's end, and asked if he was ready to go back.

But Saul showed up, plopping down across from them and planting his hamlike forearms on the table. "I talked to Mama," he said to Cissy. "She's coming back tomorrow to get Miss Caro's room ready."

Cissy immediately perked up. "What did she say?"

"She got all excited 'bout you maybe giving her lessons and asked me to invite you over on Sunday.

I checked and saw both you and the hubby are scheduled off.'' Saul cast a glance at Jack. ''You're invited to tag along, of course.''

How flattering to know he was on the ''A'' list, Jack thought as he watched Cissy eagerly nod. But any invitation was better than none, so he smiled and thanked Saul.

They chatted a while about Jack and Cissy's opinions of Bonnie, the buffet, their co-workers. It was all Jack could do to stifle his yawns. He was ready to hit the sack.

When one of the yawns escaped, Saul smiled, said he was tuckered out, too and got up and left.

On the drive back, Jack asked Cissy if she'd like some pointers on how to handle Faraday.

''There's nothing to handle.'' He heard annoyance in her voice. ''He'll forget about me by morning.''

''You heard Terry. He's taken a special liking to you.''

''You make that sound like a dirty word.''

Jack chuckled. ''To Hawke, it is.''

With sunset had come a wind that cavorted through Cissy's hair, and she buried her hands into each temple to hold it back. But the locks tumbled around her high cheekbones nonetheless, and the streetlights glowed through the strands, casting dancing shadows over her face. Her parted lips shone as lusciously as ripe fruit.

She was a picture of sensuous temptation, and Jack felt a shudder low in his belly. He looked away, and his next sentence came out harsher than he'd intended.

"You don't stand a chance around him, Cissy. He eats innocent little girls like you for breakfast."

"What makes you think I'm so innocent?" she asked defensively. "I've been around some. I know the score."

"Right," he said. "With men who think holding hands on the first date is the height of boldness."

Cissy felt a jolt of outrage. What made Jack think she had no experience? Was she wearing some kind of sign on her back or something? She'd shared some mighty passionate kisses, even some light petting, before she'd met Ed. But, she had to admit it, even though she'd never tell Jack—she and Ed had dated over a dozen times before he'd first kissed her. A chaste kiss at that.

Jack had hit the nail all right. She wasn't equipped to handle savvy, lecherous men like Hawke Faraday. But she was a quick study. She could learn.

She tilted her chin decisively. "Stay out of it, Jack. I've told you before, I can—"

"Take care of myself," Jack finished.

"You got it. Now don't forget again."

By the time they reached the cabana, Cissy was worked up. She stormed directly inside, unlocking the door and leaving it open for Jack, who was taking his sweet old time getting up the walkway.

Which drew no complaints from her. Earlier, Cissy had stashed her ferociously protected shoulder bag inside the room's only closet. Now she had to figure out what to do with the voice-activated reel-to-reel recorder and eavesdropping devices it contained.

Once she planted the bugs, she couldn't leave the recorder where Jack might hear the reels turning.

She was still inspecting the closet's skimpy proportions, when Jack finally appeared.

"I'll keep my stuff in here," she said, before he'd even crossed the threshold. She then pointed to a free-standing clothes rack. "You can have that."

"There's not enough room," he complained.

"Well, the closet won't hold everything, either."

Jack closed the front door. To avoid the bed, he squeezed close to Cissy. Too close. As he peered into the closet, his vest brushed her back and she could actually feel his body heat. She inhaled sharply, getting another whiff of his scent. For an instant, she felt light-headed, and a funny noise escaped her lips.

"You okay?" Jack gave her a quick glance.

"Just tired." Which wasn't far from the truth. She hadn't been this exhausted since she'd refused her family's help and moved herself from one apartment to another in a single day.

Satisfied, Jack returned his attention to the closet space. "It is pretty small."

His voice carried disturbing reverberations, and when he scratched his head, causing the silver eagles to tinkle, Cissy found that sound equally disturbing. Flustered, she inched aside.

"Didn't Saul say we have a storage shed out back?" Jack asked. Cissy said yes and he looked at her again. "Why are you hugging the door? I've already promised I won't attack you."

"Don't be silly. I already told you I'm just tired. I think I'll get off my feet."

She walked to the chair and had just started to sit when Jack said, "We can store some of our things in the shed."

"No way!" She sprang back up. "I'm not putting my clothes out with spiders and crickets. Besides, we both need at least one private place, no matter how small."

At least she did.

"You got secrets, Cissy?" Jack teased.

"Don't you ever quit?" Alarmed, Cissy stepped forward, which brought her face-to-face with Jack's chest. She immediately moved back.

Jack's smile widened. "Is that how you're going to deal with Hawke?"

"Cut it out, Jack."

He held on to his knowing smile, but to Cissy's relief he returned to their original subject. "Okay. You can have the closet. I'll need an extra drawer though."

"But—oh, all right. Now do you mind letting me by?"

Jack moved aside and Cissy again inspected the space. An overhead shelf held extra blankets and pillows. She pointed to them. "Why don't you use those for your bedroll?"

Jack frowned, but took the bedding down anyway. He then carried it to the empty spot on the floor. As he spread out the blanket, he grumbled, "First the bed, now the closet."

Barely concealing her triumphant grin, Cissy busied herself with setting up claim to the closet. So Jack thought she couldn't handle Hawke Faraday, did he? This showed what little he knew. After all, look how well she'd handled him.

Cissy felt like she was in a whirlwind, searching for the peaceful eye. Three days of slaving in the stables, ferreting out wedding secrets, dealing with Jack's never-ending sarcasm had stretched her thin. Anticipation of the upcoming visit with Saul and Mama Coolidge was all that kept her going.

She wanted sleep. Now. At this very moment. But she had to prepare the reel-to-reel recorder. With a weary sigh, she dug through a pile of shoes and dirty clothes, pulled out the recorder and checked its battery pack, feeling better when she saw it turning. So much rode on this story. Not just her future at *Top of the Rock,* but everything she'd ever believed about herself.

Shards of the past flashed through her mind: her brothers laughing on a tree limb as she struggled to climb it with her chunky little legs; her parents keeping her on a pony long after she was old enough for a horse; playground teachers mistaking her for a first-grader as late as the fifth grade; a former boss denying her a courthouse beat, saying no one would trust a reporter who looked like a teenager.

She'd be thirty in the fall and so far nothing had changed. Everyone still acted as if she had years to go before she finally grew up. Now she had a new chance to prove what she was made of.

Still, getting everything done with Jack around wasn't easy. The husbands and wives of the kitchen staff usually waited for their spouses at night and it would look especially odd if Cissy didn't wait for Jack.

So it had come to this. Forced to steal moments before the lunch and dinner hours when she was often so hungry she could barely concentrate.

Ignoring her growling stomach, she switched off the recorder and picked up a small plastic zip bag. Inside were the electronic miracles that she would plant at Saul and Mama's on Sunday. Wireless bugs with a range of several miles, they were smaller than Cissy's thumbnail, but powerful....

Pulling back her slipping mind, she put the reel-to-reel inside one of her empty suitcases then shoved it to the back of the closet. Just as she hovered between squatting and standing, she heard the front door open and saw a pair of nubuck hiking boots.

"Jack!" She fell back to her knees and stuffed the plastic bag into the toe of an upturned shoe. "What are you doing here?"

"Ron sent me on an errand," he said, referring to his boss. "So I decided to bring these home while I was at it." He jiggled a sack, from which poked a small pot, some bananas and the lid of a can of coffee. "Why are you crawling around down there?"

"Looking for my other tennis shoe." Cissy lifted one, which had luckily been beneath her hand, then looked at his sack. Had she spied a muffin in there? "We aren't supposed to have food in the room, Jack."

"Everyone does it. Wouldn't you like coffee first thing in the morning?"

Her stomach growled as she nodded. "Is that a muffin?"

"Several." He pulled one out. "Want it?"

"Thanks." She scrambled to her feet and greedily took it from his hand.

As Cissy peeled the wrapper off the muffin, Jack squinted into the closet. "What a mess. No wonder you can never find anything." He turned away and walked to the rickety table.

Cissy chomped on the muffin as delicately as possible considering she was near starvation, wondering why Jack was scowling. He answered the question by waving a couple of hair rollers at her.

"What do you suggest I do with all this stuff? I want to put the coffeepot here."

He swept his hand above the surface of the table. Hair rollers, yes, a dozen of them or so. And a small mirror, a tube of mascara, a pair of mismatched socks. Cissy grinned sheepishly, pretty sure some bobby pins were thrown in there for good measure.

Putting aside the muffin, Cissy hurried over and began gathering up the rollers. In the meanwhile, Jack put down the sack and surveyed the room.

Since they were seldom there at the same time, Cissy hadn't looked at the room through Jack's eyes before. Now her gaze drifted to the clothes rack where his jeans and shirts hung in precisely spaced increments. Images of his shaving supplies, lined up like little soldiers, and of his meticulously folded towel, came to mind.

He eyed the unmade bed, its covers twisting around her forgotten pajamas and bathrobe, then moved on to the bra she'd rejected that morning and left dangling from a half-open drawer.

"Reminds me of Stevie," he said, clearly struggling with annoyance.

"Who?" Cissy asked blankly, a flush creeping to her cheeks.

"My younger brother. We shared a room for a while." Sounding like the memory pained him, he raised a camisole from a pile of clothing on the back of a chair. "The stuff was different, but the ambience is similar."

"Oh." Deciding she'd better clear things out in a hurry, Cissy pulled the front of her shirt forward and began scooping objects into the basket it made. After filling the depression to the brim, she shuffled toward the bathroom.

"Dumping it all on the counter won't solve anything," Jack informed her evenly. It hadn't taken Cissy long to learn that this particular tone meant he was trying to control his temper, and for some reason that irked her more than outright scorn.

She turned. Several rollers fell onto the floor, bounced a few times, landed at Jack's feet.

"See what you made me do?" Her embarrassment rapidly turned to touchiness. "You're treating me like a bothersome child."

"Well?" Again his eyes swept the cluttered room.

Without another word, Cissy bounded into the bathroom and emptied her cargo on the counter, ignoring the items that fell into the sink. Then she finished clearing the table and repeated the process. When the table was empty, she started in on her clothes, gathering them up and throwing them into the closet.

"Now you'll never find your other tennis shoe, Cissy." Appearing suddenly behind her, Jack bent and picked up a wad of clothing. "Here," he said. "Let me show you."

With a sweep of his foot, he pushed Cissy's jumble of shoes to one side. She stifled a yelp, terrified he had exposed or damaged the bugs, but the shoe slid without tumbling. Still recovering from the fright of a lifetime, she stared mutely as Jack dropped clothes on the now-empty space.

"Lump all your whites together," he instructed, letting fall a pair of pale-colored jeans. "Oops, this is a delicate, even though it's white." He dangled her satin panty and deposited it in another spot with a grin, turning next to a burgundy shirt. "And, obviously, this is a colored."

By now Cissy was gaping in shock.

"If you sort everything as soon as it's dirty, then you don't have to do it on laundry day. It's just logic, really."

Dear God, Cissy thought, *how superior he acts.* He was treating her exactly like her older sisters and brothers once had, and she wanted to puncture his pompous balloon with a burst of rage. But that would only convince him she really was a bothersome child.

It wouldn't be easy—a blistering furnace was wanting to explode through the top of her head—but she could do it. She'd stay cool, calm, collected, politely thank Jack for his advice.

"How nice," she purred, just as she had planned.

The next line sort of slipped out. "You'll make some-one a wonderful wife."

"Better than you, Tinker Bell." His amused smile looked genuine. "Better than you." Then he touched her arm. "Come on. I'll drive you to dinner."

She saw then that Jack was completely unaware of her anger. One more person who denied her the re-spect she deserved. She couldn't win.

Well, she thought, they'd all see soon enough. When the Faraday wedding story hit the front page of *Top of the Rock* with her byline above it, they'd show new respect.

She would succeed. Absolutely. Not even the hounds of hell could stop her.

6

What a way to spend a Saturday night, Jack thought, as he crawled along a grass-and-gravel route toward the Coolidge's cottage. He buried wire as he moved, fervently wishing for wireless devices. But high-priced bugs would have to wait for more prosperous days. In the meantime, he'd use the means at hand.

He'd been given a lucky break when Cissy insisted he use the storage room, even though it had seemed unfair at the time. Since she had no reason to go there, he didn't have to worry about her accidentally discovering the recorder from which the wire originated. For, if a way existed to discover it, he felt sure Cissy would find it. She noticed everything and asked tons of questions.

Although, he realized with a jab of peevishness, her curiosity seldom extended to him. She never even asked why he left the cabana every night. A good thing, too, he'd often told himself, otherwise he'd have to come up with all kinds of excuses every time he wanted to transcribe his tapes.

A cloud slid over the moon just then, and Jack hastily buried the remaining wire and hurried to the wall of the cottage while he still had the cover of darkness. He then listened for sounds within and, hearing none, began stringing the wire behind a bush, inching it toward the window. With great care, he then slid the end of the wire underneath the frame of the screen. When he was satisfied it was secure, he smiled happily.

Come tomorrow, it would be an easy matter to open the inside window and connect the bug. The Faraday wedding story would soon be his.

Sunday couldn't come soon enough for Cissy. She'd been so impatient, she barely made it through the day. But finally, with the bugs securely in her pocket, she and Jack were on Saul's doorstep being introduced to Mama.

"Hello." Speaking with a trace of a Caribbean accent, Saul's bride extended a welcoming hand, and her demeanor surprised Cissy. She'd expected someone as down-home as Saul, but this woman was tall and slim, as regal as an African princess, and her simple greeting made Cissy feel as if she were being presented to royalty.

Smothering her enthusiasm, Cissy extended her hand, and returned Mama's greeting with equal reserve, noticing that Jack also responded with a measure of aloofness.

They were then ushered inside the cottage, and Cissy glanced around with a twinge of envy as she took in the greater luxury afforded to the ranch's permanent staff. Space. Lots of space. They even had a bedroom.

As if that wasn't enough, new, obviously expensive, furniture was tastefully arranged over a colorful room-size rug that exposed a border of polished wood. A circular rattan game table sat in one corner, and it was here that they were led.

A splashy lazy Susan, filled with exquisite hors d'oeuvres, occupied the center of the table, and a bottle of wine was chilling in a silver ice bucket. A far cry from the beer and pretzels Cissy had expected.

As Saul held out a chair for her, Cissy sneaked a glance at a closed door to her left, which she assumed was the bedroom. Sometime during the evening she had to find a way in there.

When they were all seated, Mama poured the wine, told Jack and Cissy to help themselves from the lazy Susan, then leaned toward Cissy. "Saul tells me you're a horsewoman."

"Yes, I am."

Mama went on to ask about Cissy's experience, and so she mentioned her childhood on the ranch, then dredged up some resort names from the phony résumé JoJo had provided Bonnie Katchum. As the questions grew more probing, Cissy realized they probably wouldn't be spending a chatty evening talking about the wedding. After a while, as she struggled not to squirm in her elegant rattan chair, she heard Saul tap his fingers on the table.

"Now, now, Mama," he said. "Cissy's offered you a favor. You're talking like you think she might swipe Miss Caro's jewels."

"Of course. I'm so used to grilling the upstairs maids—Miss Caro leaves that to me." She smiled proudly. "Some of the girls I get, well, you wouldn't believe.'' She reached over and patted Cissy's hand. ''Forgive me. I do appreciate your offer.''

Cissy nodded and asked Mama about her previous riding experience, giving some tips on problems the woman brought up. Everyone relaxed, and soon Saul put aside the food and brought out a Monopoly board. Cissy took advantage of the momentary confusion to peel the back off one of the bugs and stick it to the brace of the table. She then pitched in with setting up the game. About halfway through the setup, Jack asked for the bathroom.

Saul pointed to the door Cissy had noticed earlier. ''It's inside the bedroom.''

Cissy could have kissed Jack for so neatly solving her problem. When he came back, she smiled at him approvingly, which he returned with a puzzled look.

Then the game began and grew lively. Mama played with all the gusto of a land baron, and Cissy was seen groaning as she completed her turn by paying her hostess rent on Park Place.

''Drown your sorrows, Cissy?'' Saul asked, lifting the wine bottle.

''Thanks, but I've had too much already.'' She hooked a thumb toward the bedroom door. ''May I?''

Saul nodded. As she left the room, she heard the roll of Jack's dice. Loosen up, she told herself, she had plenty of time. But as she closed the bedroom door behind her, her heart thrummed like a tom-tom. She was scared to death, not to mention a little guilty about deceiving her hosts, but she was also thrilled.

The big time was within her grasp. She patted the watch pocket of her jeans, then pulled out the contents. All she had to do was follow instructions and her little bugs would do the rest.

As expected, the room had a phone. She followed the cord to the wall jack, then knelt and pulled it out. With trembling hands, she wedged a bug in the U of the plastic jack, then reconnected it. From here, she'd been told, it would pick up conversations from any phone in the house.

She'd been hoping for a headboard to put the second bug behind, but the bed had none. So where? Behind the taffeta drapes? Beneath the oak bed stand? She backed up to view the rest of the room and heard a sudden noise.

An explosion! Or at least that's how it seemed. Her overworked heart skipped a beat, then resumed in double-time.

No matter what her runaway imagination said, Cissy knew she'd only heard a rustle, and she turned to seek the source. Something swished again. Shoving back a gasp, she jumped like she was under sniper fire.

Just as she realized she'd been brushing against the skirt of the taffeta bedspread, the bug flew from her hand. In horror, she watched it strike the earth-toned carpet and bounce several times.

Cissy scrambled after it.

It had disappeared.

Her mouth went dry. She burned holes in the carpet with her eyes, saw nothing. Dropping to her knees, she crawled around the bed, rubbing her fingers over the carpet, flinching each time she disturbed the quiet folds of the bedspread.

How far could it have gone? The floor hadn't simply swallowed it up. Her searching grew more and more frantic, and she was nearly clawing at the fibers when she heard the bedroom doorknob turn.

"It's your turn, Cissy," boomed Jack's baritone voice. The door swung slowly open, giving entrance to a stream of light. Cissy sprang to her feet.

"Jack!" She forced her frozen face into a semblance of a smile. "My turn? Already? That didn't take long, did it? I've only been gone a minute. No, no siree, not long at all."

Jack scowled. "What're you doing, Cissy? You shouldn't be nosing through Saul and Mama's bedroom."

"Nosing? I am *not* nosing. I, uh, I dropped my lipstick, that's all. And it rolled over here. Can you imagine that? *All* the way over here. But I found it." Cissy fished into a shirt pocket, then waved her lipstick at Jack like a prize. "Yep, I found it. See?"

The lines in Jack's forehead deepened, and he walked over until he stood mere inches away.

"You've been acting funny all night. Are you okay?" He put his hands on her shoulders and touched her forehead with his. "Nope, no fever."

Cissy's jitters instantly vanished. She felt weary. Very, very weary. The week had been long, full of tension. For one self-indulgent second, she allowed herself to lean on Jack.

"I'm fine," she said in a thready voice. "Really I am."

"This act we've been putting on," he asked gently. "Is it getting to you?"

Cissy wanted to groan. What was this? Jack was never nice to her.

"It is bothering you!"

Cissy steeled herself for another lie. "It *is* harder than I expected."

"For me, too," he confessed.

"We'd better get back to the game." Feeling ashamed, she looked down, then moved away. She'd leaned long enough.

"Right, they're waiting for your play." Jack turned to leave the room. Cissy moved to follow, eyes still downcast, and caught a glint of metal in the splash of light from the other room.

She checked to make sure Jack wasn't watching, then furtively lifted the bedspread and nudged the bug with her foot. It rolled under the bed.

Mission accomplished, she thought, even though she'd nearly died from fright. She just hoped Mama didn't vacuum under there very often.

7

When Jack rolled over the next morning, his hand struck a hard, unfriendly floor. Shocked awake, he sprang to a sitting position, rubbed his eyes and blinked a few times, then looked hazily at the clock. He might as well get up; it was about to go off anyway.

Sleeping on the floor had turned him into a sack of aching muscles and, still weary, he gazed with longing at the bed Cissy had left. Unmade as usual, it called to him and he longed to climb beneath its cool, inviting sheets.

Jack had worked as a fry cook in high school and had been a sous chef at a four-star restaurant during college, but he'd never cooked for such multitudes before. It would take at least another week to get up to speed. Meanwhile, he sacrificed sleep in order to transcribe his tapes, and the few hours he got on this bed of nails—well, he exaggerated, the floor didn't actually have nails—weren't much better than no sleep at all.

With a muffled groan, he got up, padded to the bathroom and turned on the shower. Ten steaming minutes later, he felt human again. He towel-dried his hair and rubbed his stiff muscles briskly, then returned to the bedroom to dress.

As he was shoving dirty clothes into a laundry bag, he surveyed the mess Cissy left behind. The bedclothes were tangled. A T-shirt hung from her bureau drawer. Her pajamas dangled from the bathroom doorknob. The locations of her clothing were endless and imaginative. Everywhere except the piles he'd made in the closet.

Begrudgingly, he began gathering her silky things, subliminally aware that each piece emanated a fragrance he'd already come to associate with her.

Usually he just dumped her clothes outside the closet door, but this time, for some reason he couldn't explain, he sorted them, and the gesture made him unaccountably angry.

He was becoming Cissy's housemaid. And a regular nag, too. This had to stop, he thought, although how he'd stop it was another matter altogether.

When he finished that thankless task, Jack locked up and headed for the golf cart. What was it about Cissy? he asked himself as he walked. Somehow he always ended up fretting about her. Like the night before, when she'd stayed in Saul's bathroom so long. Of course, he'd originally gone in there because he feared she'd somehow come across the bug he'd planted. But when the light from the front room had spilled on her face, he'd seen her weariness and had realized she'd been visibly tense all night.

He climbed into the cart and considered that he might somehow be the cause of Cissy's tension. He often felt as if he were exploiting her, and the feeling didn't sit well with him. She wasn't such a bad partner, not at all, and lately he'd found that he almost liked having her around. Despite her flippant mouth, sloppy ways and resistance to all his efforts to steer her right, Cissy Benton was okay.

While driving to the house, Jack grew uncomfortably aware that he enjoyed complaining about those quirks of hers. Kind of like old married folks.

Get a grip, man. It's only a make-believe marriage.

Yeah, he grumbled to himself, if it were real, he'd be sleeping in Cissy's soft bed instead of on the hard floor.

With that thought, Jack pulled up to the house, got out of the cart and headed for work, determined to keep his mind off Cissy for the rest of the day.

Cissy had her own problems. Piles and piles of horse poo. While Jack slept, she'd been raking stalls. Now all the horsey residue had to be loaded into a wheelbarrow a shovelful at a time.

Her arms and back ached, and Tiny wasn't cutting her any slack. He sent her for hundred-pound sacks of grain just as quickly as he did the men. She'd always wanted to be recognized for her abilities, but at times Tiny made her yearn for Jack's more gentlemanly ways.

Where was Jack Cook now?

Cooking, of course.

Why hadn't she learned to cook? Then she'd be in the cool main house and he'd be here shoveling—

She wasn't being fair, of course. She should offer to trade nights in the bed, but her every muscle screamed with protest, and even the *idea* of sleeping on the floor made her cringe. A day in the barn left her almost too tired to eat, let alone to pick up after herself.

Jack's nagging didn't help. After that sweet little lesson on laundry etiquette, she'd found herself getting perverse pleasure from being sloppier than ever.

But then he'd done that *thing* last night. Why had he gone all warm and fuzzy on her? She'd grown used to his sarcasm. She could handle it. But this about-face, well, it threw her off balance. Look how guilty she felt pulling one over on Saul and Mama. What if Jack turned nice? Really, really nice. What if she began to—

"Cissy, you done with that manure?" Tiny asked from another row of stalls.

"Almost."

"Good. Next, go get that stallion and exercise him on a line."

Cissy felt like crying. The stallion almost killed her Saturday. Now it was getting a second chance. As she toted away the last load of manure, she remembered what Jack had said about gaining weight from all the food. What had ever made her think being a wrangler on a rock star's ranch would be easy?

She'd been wrong. Jack had been right. Again.

That's what made her the maddest.

He was right just too damned often.

"Dave Jordon's come up," Saul said.

"Just super," grumbled a balding man. "He'll probably put us in uniforms this time."

Cissy lowered herself gingerly into a cramped spot between Saul and the bald guy and wearily studied her overflowing plate. Torn between starvation, the desire to sleep for the next year and the conversation, she opted for the food.

As she gulped down some stew—the work was making her ravenous—Saul looked over. "You should chew more. Twenty times is best. Least that's what Mama says."

Cissy swallowed, smiled. "True. I'm probably ruining my digestion."

"Well, I don' know. I ate fast for a long time before she came along, and never got ulcers." He chuckled. "She says it hasn't caught up with me yet."

Deciding eating was now out of the question—Saul did love to talk, so she might as well take advantage of it—Cissy clicked on her recorder. "Do you know Dave Jordon?" she asked.

"I always fetch him from the airport but can't say I really know him. He's a man on the go. Takes right good care of Mr. Hawke though.... Oops, 'cuse me, Cissy. There's Mama." Saul squiggled out of his cramped seat and went to meet his wife.

So much for Dave Jordon, Cissy thought. Too tired to care, she returned to the stew, nearly inhaling it, and watched Saul escort his wife through the food line. Mama was wearing a crisp black-and-white uniform that set her apart from her co-workers, and Cissy didn't know if she wore it as a preference or to remind the others that she worked personally for Caro.

As the previous evening had shown, Mama could be a bit snobbish. As the Monopoly game progressed, however, she began discussing the wedding, telling Cissy about the bridesmaids and even making a drawing of the wedding dress. Although aware that the dress was already plastered over the newspapers, Cissy still saw it as a sign the woman was beginning to trust her.

But only so far. When Saul blurted out that Hawke's lead drummer called the wedding a farce and refused to be best man, Mama had said, "Hush!"

Cissy smiled now as the subject of her thoughts approached, carrying a plate of food. Mama greeted her warmly, but her expression said she expected Cissy to give up her seat. Arranging her features into a stoic expression, Cissy grabbed her dinner and eased off the bench. Wandering among the tables, she stopped now and then to say hello to someone, unable to find an empty seat. Eventually she moved to the lattice fence and leaned, figuring that standing was better anyway.

When she'd finished eating, she ditched her dinnerware and meandered into the lovely brick courtyard behind the fence. Somewhere in there a padded lounge awaited her, and she was eagerly anticipating that pleasure when she walked into the dim courtyard. She stopped to let her eyes adjust.

"Hi, honey."

Cissy recognized the voice immediately. Unpleasant shivers raced down her spine. As her eyes got used to the dark, she saw Hawke Faraday silhouetted on one of the loungers. He got up and walked toward her. "What brings you here?" His words broadcasted the smell of gin.

Cissy stepped back involuntarily.

"Waiting for my husband." She waved her rings and took another backward step. What was wrong with her? This was a perfect opportunity to pump the star for information, but her every instinct urged her to run.

"Husband?" A sly smile appeared on Hawke's face as he moved in tandem with Cissy's steps. With his longer legs, he easily narrowed the distance between them and soon Cissy bumped into a tree trunk. Hawk closed the remaining distance. "Husbands can be inconvenient, don't you think?"

"Inconvenient?" Cissy countered blithely, trying to shrink into the tree. "You better hope not. You'll be one in... What? A couple weeks, maybe?"

"Oh, that." Hawke made a gesture of dismissal, then placed a hand beside Cissy's head. The flash of disappointment she felt about failing to glean information was instantly eclipsed by her fear she was about to be mauled. "We do things a little different in the music industry."

"Not me. I'm old-fashioned. Yep, that's me, an old-fashioned girl. Real old-fashioned. Love my husband, love kids, white picket fences, chocolate-chip cookies. Love 'em, love 'em all."

As she prattled, Hawke put his other hand on the opposite side of her head. Her gaze darted to the courtyard gate—thank God, she'd left it open—hoping to see someone she knew. Someone safe. Like Saul or Tiny. Even...

Jack. Of course. Jack. After all, he was supposed to be her husband.

"I'm just wild about Jack." Cissy forced a dreamy smile on her face. "He's made me the luckiest woman on earth. I don't know how I'd live without him."

The singer's expression softened for a moment. "I love innocence," he crooned.

At that moment, as if answering Cissy's prayers, Jack whisked by, swinging an empty tray. Never in that whole week had he looked better.

"Jack! Jack, sweetheart!" she called. Jack stopped and swiveled his head to and fro.

"There's my sweetie pie, my darling husband, the light of my life." Not caring that she sounded like a raving lunatic, she ducked under Hawke's entrapping arm and said, "Will you excuse me, Mr. Faraday?"

"Sure thing, honey. We'll make it some other time."

Not knowing how to answer, Cissy merely nodded, then dashed out of the courtyard. She felt Hawke's eyes boring into her back as she caught up with Jack.

"Sweetheart," she cooed loudly, slipping an arm around his waist. "Let me help you finish so we can get out of here and...well, you know."

"What's gotten into you, Cissy?"

"Shh," Cissy whispered. "Don't ask questions. Just put your arm around me."

"Why?" Jack raised his voice.

"We're supposed to be newlyweds," she hissed. "Remember?"

The feel of Cissy's arm around his waist was tantalizing, and Jack muttered a soft curse as he pulled her under his arm. He had no idea why she was putting on this act, but she'd been using him as a house-maid for too long, and he felt like getting even.

As she nestled sweetly against him, feeling too familiar in the crook of his arm, Jack lowered his head toward her face. Should he?

From the corner of his eye, he caught a glimpse of Faraday leaving the courtyard from which Cissy had emerged. He immediately knew the reason for her strange behavior.

He shouldn't take advantage of it. But would he? Now *that* was a different question. Allowing no time for second thoughts, he placed a kiss on her lips, fully expecting her to jerk away. Instead, her mouth softened, parted, and Jack's tongue slipped inside as if of its own volition. Her own tongue came to life, flickering against the tip of his.

Dear God! He'd done this as a joke, as gentle revenge for giving up the bed. But now, in that fleeting encounter of lips and of tongues, a place deep in his heart shifted, shuddered and remained forever moved.

Shocked, Jack pulled back and gazed on Cissy's face. Her eyes were half-closed, her lips still parted and she seemed somehow in awe.

But if she was awed, she quickly recovered. Her eyes snapped open. "Wh-wh-what did you do that for?"

"For Faraday's benefit." He let go of Cissy's shoulder. "He made another move on you, didn't he?"

"Yeah, he did. Thanks...I guess." Cissy brought her fingers to her lips and brushed them softly.

"That's what I was doing, too. Putting on a show for Faraday."

Jack wondered if that were true. Had she just taken advantage of his unexpected kiss, or had she felt the same spooky tug. That was stupid, he thought angrily. It was only a feather kiss; their tongues had barely touched. It meant nothing.

Nothing.

Still, if he had any sense at all, he'd better not kiss Cissy Benton again.

8

Cissy slithered out of the golf cart, steadying herself against the handrail before attempting to walk to the cabana. Each movement was agony.

Jack hadn't noticed. After their unsettling kiss he'd treated her with offhanded casualness, and when he was finally released from his shift, he'd spent most of his meal talking with Terry from housekeeping.

Well, who cared? All she wanted was a hot bath and a good night's sleep. She limped inside and grabbed the bathroom doorknob with visions of steaming, scented bathwater in her mind.

"Cissy, I want to talk."

Determined to be patient, she turned and regarded him with just the smallest tap of her foot.

"Look," he said. "I'm as tired in the morning as I am when I go to bed—using that term loosely—and we need to work something out. I can't continue sleeping on the floor every night."

"What do you suggest?" She unconsciously quickened the tapping of her foot.

"Drawing straws, taking turns. Whatever." He glared at the floor. "Will you *stop* that."

Cissy looked down. "Oh...." She planted her foot firmly on the floor, then moved her gaze to Jack.

She had to admit he looked grim and tired, and she almost felt sorry for him. Circles darkened the tanned skin under his eyes. Strands of hair had broken loose and hung untidily around his beard-roughened jaw.

There were times Cissy wondered why a man like Jack—intelligent, articulate and apparently well educated—worked as a cook. But this wasn't one of those times. Right now she only wondered how she'd ever make it through the summer in such close quarters, when he somehow managed to look brutally sexy even when he was a total mess.

"Can I take a bath first?" she asked, wanting to escape for a while. "I feel grubby."

Jack drew his thick eyebrows into a disapproving V and blew out his breath. "Okay. But don't take too long."

"Why, sir, how gallant."

Jack's frown deepened, but Cissy was simply too frazzled to care, and seconds later, as she poured bubble bath beneath the pouring faucet, she forgot all about it.

Initially, the sweet-smelling water did little to relax her. Men! She had no idea what to do with them. Although her mixed feelings for Jack sometimes troubled her, she still felt a measure of control. He behaved so much like her older brothers. It mitigated the itsy-bitsy attraction she felt for him and convinced her he felt none for her.

Hawke was another matter. The rock star saw her as an innocent, which certainly wasn't protection. He didn't care about her lack of experience or her vows to Jack, only about his conquest. She needed some other approach to fend him off.

Think of those forties movies, all those glamorous women. The thought came out of nowhere, an answer to Cissy's prayers. Joan Crawford, Barbara Stanwyck, Bette Davis. Those witty retorts, that self-possession. She needed those qualities and, by golly, she'd find a way to get them. She'd come across as wise and knowing, a woman to be reckoned with, and convince Hawke she had his number and didn't plan to dial it unless he measured up.

She could do that, yes she could. And thus challenged, Hawke would find a more gullible victim.

This decision calmed Cissy's turmoil, but she again became aware of her aching body. She shifted to inspect her gluteus maximus. An angry purple bruise covered the entire area and seeped down her thigh. One more problem among many. Well, she wouldn't be wearing shorts for a while, but otherwise it looked like no harm was done. She closed her eyes and leaned back, allowing the water to wash away her pain.

Pretty soon she was dreaming of a tall, broad-shouldered man with long hair the color of deep, rich wood; it was held back by a strip of leather with silver ornaments. He was kissing her. She was kissing him back.

Oh, boy, was she kissing him....

Cissy awoke to a tub of frigid water. Shivering, she climbed out, quickly rubbed herself dry, then wrapped up in a thick terry-cloth robe. As she secured the tie, fragments of the dream returned and a flush crept up her face. The man had looked remarkably like Jack, the kiss began remarkably like the one on the patio. Only, this time she had responded with uninhibited passion.

How was she supposed to go out and face Jack after a dream like that?

Well, no getting around it. He was out there, waiting, wanting to talk about the bed, about where she'd sleep, about where *he'd* sleep. Bracing herself, Cissy opened the door, expecting to see Jack impatiently pacing the room.

But the lights were dim, the room blessedly quiet, empty. Assuming Jack must have gone for his usual evening walk, and more relieved than she wanted to admit, she padded across the room to the dresser. After pulling out her pajamas, she shrugged off the robe and let it drop to the floor.

Maybe it was the noise made by the closing drawer that roused Jack from his place beneath the rumpled bedcovers. He wasn't sure. But as he peeked above the edge of the blanket, he saw Cissy. She faced away from him, a vision of naked curves and tousled curls. A fresh talcum scent floated toward him, enveloping his senses, and his breath stopped somewhere in the region of his heart. Entranced, he stayed very still, ignoring his better judgment that told him he was treading on thin ice.

She reached up to put on her silky nightshirt, and he followed the curvatures of her arms, her gently sloping shoulders, her firm and creamy back. As she stepped into a pair of matching briefs, his eyes moved to her tiny feet and slim ankles, continued up the hills and valleys of her shapely legs and ended at the firm, round flesh of her fanny....

"My God, Cissy! What happened to you?"

Hastily jerking up the pajama bottoms, Cissy spun around.

"Why the hell are you spying on me?"

"I wasn't spying!" Jack answered irritably, trying to disguise his embarrassment. "You took so long, I fell asleep. Now, where did you get that bruise?" He got up and took hold of Cissy's slender shoulder. Leaning over, he ran his other hand gently over the purple mark beneath the pajama hem. *Judas Priest, who had marred Cissy's beautiful skin this way?*

Cissy jerked away, startled by Jack's outburst and by the electrifying jolt his touch had caused. She was also a little frightened, although she wasn't sure why. Clearly, Jack didn't mean to hurt her. If anything, he acted... What?

Concerned.

Too concerned. Possessively concerned. She felt a rush of déjà vu. That was how it started with Ed. First he'd wanted to champion her with her co-workers, then he began advising her on her career. Before she knew it, Ed was running her life and she felt like she'd never left home. She hadn't realized the cost until she'd turned down a promising overseas assignment. She never got another offer.

Well, she wasn't about to let Jack move into that empty role. Uh-uh, no way.

"It's not your problem," she said shortly. Feeling

claustrophobic in the narrow space between the bed and dresser, she inched away, then leaned over and picked up her robe. "So don't trouble yourself."

"I can't help caring if you're hurt, Cissy!" Jack's vehemence startled her. He'd give her no rest until she admitted the embarrassing truth.

"Hawke's damned stallion kicked me this morning," she admitted sheepishly, slipping into her robe and knotting the tie.

"Oh." Jack's face softened, formed into a confused frown.

"What did you think happened?"

"I don't know." Jack paused and looked away. "After seeing what happened with Faraday tonight, I wasn't so sure things would be any different in the barn."

Cissy laughed. "They treat me like one of the boys."

"Is that funny?"

"If they treated me more like a woman, I wouldn't have been handling that stallion. I think Tiny is testing me. That's the meanest horse in all kingdom come."

"I'll ask him to give that horse to someone else. You're too small to work with vicious animals."

"No!" There! He was already starting! Cissy leaned forward and tapped Jack's collarbone. "I can handle anything Tiny dishes out, Jack. Why can't you get that? Why can't you stop interfering?"

"Not interfering, Cissy, helping! Everyone needs watching over from time to time." He enclosed her finger with his hand, holding it close to his heart, and his heated words melted Cissy's annoyance. Then, more softly, he added, "Even you."

Cissy shivered and pulled her finger away. "Please, Jack, I know you mean well. But your help isn't needed. Really."

Burying her hands in the pockets, she huddled inside her robe and tried to conjure up a grateful smile. She could only manage a wan grin. The combination of Hawke's unwelcome advances, Jack's astonishingly welcome kiss, the disturbing dream and her aching hip thoroughly befuddled her. All she knew for sure was she wanted some sleep. She walked to the bed and eased down.

"Do you still want to talk about who gets the bed?"

Jack smiled with chagrin. "I'd be a real heel to put you on the floor tonight."

"Do what you think is right."

Jack looked at the blankets stacked in the corner. Wearing a pained expression, he walked wearily over to pick them up. "You keep the bed for now, but as soon as that bruise heals, you're bunking with these on alternate nights."

"Fair enough." Cissy slipped out of her robe, pulled back the covers and gratefully crawled underneath them.

"Think nothing of it," Jack said dryly, disappearing into the bathroom.

I won't. Cissy scrunched down into the bed.

"Eee-a-ouch!" Sparks of pain shot through her hip and leg.

Jack poked his head into the room. "Ice would help."

"Unfortunately, we don't have any, and I'm too tired to go out."

Jack crossed the room, got a towel from one of his dresser drawers, then went outside. Although curious about his destination, Cissy floated on the edge of sleep. Just as she was about to surrender, he came back.

"Try this." He lifted the blanket and placed a cool bundle against her bruise. She reached back, feeling a growing-too-disturbingly-familiar shock as she brushed his retreating hand and struck a towel-covered object.

He'd made an ice bag. For her. Hot tears filled her eyes. Her voice clutched. "Thanks."

"No problem." In seconds, his footsteps retreated, the bathroom door clicked shut. Cissy closed her eyes, waiting for blessed sleep. But it didn't come. A few minutes later Jack reentered. A light switch snapped, and she heard him arranging his blankets. As the cool pack soothed her throbbing bruise, she thought about how uncomfortable he must be on the unyielding floor.

"Jack," she whispered through the darkness. "Why don't you bring your blankets up here?"

He didn't answer, but his bedclothes stirred the air, and soon she felt the mattress shift from his weight.

"Good night, Cissy," he said softly.

"Good night."

She lay very still, her back to his. Still haunted by his impulsive kiss and the unwelcome dream, she wondered if she'd sleep a wink with him so near. She wanted both of those incidents out of her mind. It wouldn't hurt, either, if she could forget he was sleeping beside her altogether.

Forgetfulness was hard to come by, though, and as she drifted in and out of a fretful sleep, she fought an ever-increasing desire to slide over and cuddle against Jack's long body.

Sometime during the night Cissy's desire won. She awoke pressed against Jack's back, one arm thrown across his bare waist.

She jerked away and was stopped short by her bruised bottom. Stifling a groan, she eased upright, gingerly avoiding the injured buttock. Thus situated— and since Jack had thrown off the blankets—she couldn't help but stare.

His dark lashes fluttered against his cheekbones, and his sculptured lips, softened by sleep, parted with a sigh. Muffling a gasp, Cissy looked away. He shifted slightly, then settled down again. A few seconds passed before Cissy dared looked back.

She'd never seen Jack this way before.

Half-naked.

Loosened from its usual restraint, his mahogany hair fell in a luxuriant sheet over one shoulder, and his tanned chest and stomach rose and fell rhythmically. A thin strip of white skin streaked his hipbones, and dark hair curled below his navel to disappear beneath the band of his briefs.

Cissy reached out, her hand hovering millimeters above him. Was his skin as velvety smooth as it looked? Were the muscles as hard? If she gave in to the urge to stroke him, would he delight in the sensations her fingertips created?

He stirred again and she emitted a small squeak, jerked her hand away.

What nonsense, she told herself, angrily throwing her legs over the bed. Her hip gave a punishing jab, which she somehow felt was no more than she deserved for her foolishness.

Later, fresh from a shower and wrapped in her fluffy robe, she rummaged through her drawers, shoving aside haphazard piles of knit shirts and underwear to find a match to the sock in her hand. She needed to get organized. Jack never had this problem, and at times she admired his tiresome orderliness.

As she struggled with a shirt that was slipping from her grasp, she saw the piles on the floor. Not that she hadn't seen them before, but he usually just dumped the clothes in a heap.

This time he'd sorted them. Whites with whites, delicates with delicates and so on, exactly the way he'd instructed her. Perhaps he was once again hinting that she keep up with her laundry. But maybe not.

She thought about all his subtle, thoughtful ways. The coffeepot and goodies he'd brought to the room. The ice pack he fetched last night, his gallant relinquishing of the bed. Had she struggled so long to be independent that she'd forgotten how sweet a little tenderness could be?

Lifting her eyes toward Jack's sleeping form, she felt somehow as if she were caressing him. She drank in the contrast of his dark hair against the pillowcase, drank in the shadows and highlights playing over the angles of his muscles.

A sweet warmth rushed through her body, and she wanted to cross the room and finish the kiss they'd started the night before. With a thrust of will, she didn't. But as she entered the bathroom to dress, she still felt the warmth.

So this time, instead of leaving her soggy towels on the tile floor, instead of leaving her pajamas crumpled in a corner, she picked them up, carried them to the piles and sorted them.

Whites with whites, delicates with delicates. And so on.

As the door clicked shut, Jack's eyes snapped open. Had Cissy really been devouring him with her eyes? He shook his head with a bemused smile. Of course not. Just an outrageous dream, and even more reason to regret leaving the bed.

He lay there awhile, staring at the ceiling. What was going through his sleep-fogged mind? He had one purpose for being here, and only one. He couldn't afford to let Cissy get under his skin. This juncture of his life left no room for distractions.

Michelle had shown him how difficult relationships could be. Not that the transparent Cissy resembled his devious ex-girlfriend in any way, but because of her, he hadn't even gone over his tapes last night.

Maybe later, when *Movers & Shakers* gained solid ground, he'd look Cissy up....

No way, Jack, he told himself. *Put it out of your mind.*

He combed his fingers through his hair, then headed for the shower. When he finished his morning routine, he sat down in one of the shabby chairs and began playing tapes.

Terry, the cynical brunette, was a wealth of information. Too bad her accuracy was questionable. Mama remained a promising source, but tended to clam up when pressed for details. Who knew how long it would take to loosen her up? His best chance was to get close to Dave Jordon—no easy task for a third-string cook.

As these choices ran through his head, Jack listened to his recording, making periodic notes until he reached the end. After labeling the tape, he put it inside the jacket, which he also labeled, then filed in a black carrying case that already held more than a dozen other tapes.

Casting a glance at his watch, he saw he'd used up more time than he thought, which rattled him. He hurriedly picked up the cassette case to put it away.

"Damn!"

He'd forgotten to secure the lid. Despite his clumsy attempt to stop it, the base swung loose, tumbling little rectangles all over the floor. Jack scooped them up quickly and dumped them back in the case, staring in dismay at the jumble. But he was out of time. The sorting would have to wait.

This time he carefully latched the lid, then carried the box to the dresser and shoved it beneath a row of underwear.

Soon he was speeding down the driveway to the main house as fast as the golf cart would go. Sprinting into the kitchen only seconds before his shift started, he suddenly remembered that his recorder was still on the table.

9

At a little after noon, Cissy hobbled to the room, aching badly, yet elated with success. Her fanny had received additional punishment from a morning horseback ride, and the friends of Caro's she'd been directed to guide had jabbered on and on about essentially nothing. Success appeared later, when Tiny instructed her to prepare two empty stalls.

"A matched pair's coming in. On loan." He scrunched his furrowed forehead until it was a mass of wrinkles, implying he didn't appreciate tending someone else's highbred horses.

The beautiful palomino pair arrived just before Cissy's lunch break. As soon as she led the first one out of the trailer, she knew exactly where the wedding would be held.

On the ranch. On horseback. With the matched pair an integral part of the wedding party. And when Cissy hefted their heavy show saddles onto storage racks, she saw she could plant bugs beneath the lush fleece linings.

She hadn't received this big a break since the star reporter on her college newspaper had taken ill, giving Cissy the opportunity to cover the speech of a presidential candidate.

Now, despite her throbbing bruise and the tug of the inviting bed, she cheerfully sat in one of the battered armchairs and reached behind her for the microrecorder in her waist pack. Setting it on her lap, she pushed a button and began talking about what she observed.

The task took about ten minutes, leaving less than an hour to hitch a ride to the main house for lunch. Cissy carefully labeled the cassette, one of the few things in her life she did religiously, then picked up the recorder to return it to her pack.

The pack resisted her attempt to slide it forward. She jerked impatiently, but it didn't budge. The task, she saw, would take both hands, so she stood up and set the recorder on the table next to the coffeepot. Finding the latch snagged on one of her belt loops, she quickly uncoupled it, then reached out to retrieve the recorder.

She blinked in disbelief.

Where had the second recorder come from?

Obviously it wasn't hers. But why would Jack need a micro? They weren't good for anything except interviews. A person didn't exactly plunk in a music tape and go jogging with a recorder like that.

Puzzled, she picked up the machine and began turning it over in her hands. The small silver label on the back pulled a gasp from her lips. *Movers & Shakers* it read, the name of a magazine if she'd ever heard one. Beneath that were a series of numbers that looked like an inventory control.

Oh, God! Oh, God! The exclamations ricocheted off the walls of her mind. Could Jack be a reporter? No, no, of course not. Her imagination was going wild again.

Then she spied a small plastic box lying near the table leg. With a sick sensation in her stomach, she leaned over and gingerly picked it up as if it were a poisonous snake. The cassette was labeled with date and content, exactly the way Cissy had been taught to label hers. She took it out, placed it in her player and pushed the play button.

''Caro is so gorgeous,'' a female voice crooned.

Her voice! She blinked angrily, fighting back tears. *Damn! Oh, damn, damn, damn.* Jack Cook *was* a reporter.

And he was after her story.

Why hadn't Cissy shown up for lunch? Jack wondered, as he cut biscuit dough into round shapes and arranged them on a baking sheet. Ignoring the disapproving glances from Ron, he'd made several trips to the patio, but hadn't seen her.

When he asked around, no one else had seen her either, but he'd been teased several times about their differing versions of their courtship. They'd better get their stories straight, he decided. But what really weighed on his mind was the fear she'd discovered his microrecorder.

Even if she found it, why would she give it any thought? He could claim he used it to record voice letters for his family, which in fact he did on occasion.

That decided, he returned to the more perilous situation of their differing stories. Eventually, someone would catch on. They had to put their heads together and get the facts straight. He'd better send a note to the stables and ask Cissy to meet him during dinner. They could eat in the quiet kitchen nook, after the food was out on the serving tables, and have some fun inventing a suitable history. She'd laugh—he was sure she would—and he loved the sound of her laugh.

Denying the surge of anticipation he felt, Jack picked up the baking sheet and carried it to the oven. As he slipped it inside, he glanced at the counter and saw a tray of shiny chocolate éclairs nestled inside lacy paper containers. Cissy loved éclairs, and complained that they usually disappeared before she ever got one. Darting a quick glance around to be sure no one was looking, Jack picked one up and took it to the cooler where he hid it behind a bag of cantaloupes.

He then grabbed a pencil and a piece of notepaper.

"Cissy," he wrote. "Come to the kitchen for dinner. I have a surprise." With a smile, he signed, "Love, Jack."

He couldn't wait to see her face when he gave her the éclair.

Cissy didn't know how long she'd stared at nothing, just that she'd used up most of her lunch hour. Not really hungry, but knowing she had to eat something, she reached out, took a banana from the basket Jack had purloined from somewhere and began listlessly peeling it.

This discovery explained a lot. Like why Jack was so eager to tag along with her to the Coolidges, why he never teased about her gushy questions, even though he did about *everything* else. And why, since that first night, he hadn't uttered a single complaint about keeping his things in the inconvenient outside storage room.

What should she do next? Telling Jack what she'd found was an option, of course. Maybe he'd confide in her and give her investigation a boost, but the sleaziness of pretending to be his friend was hard to stomach.

Although no stranger to professional competition, she'd always been open about it. She had never sneaked behind someone's back and used them. Could she do that? Was the story and its subsequent accolades that important?

Yet who would she be if she lost the story to Jack? Exactly who she'd always been—little Cissy Benton, the tiny blond fluff ball. That was just as hard to stomach.

Taking a bite of banana she didn't really want, Cissy decided her first order of business was to learn where Jack stored his tapes.

She searched under the bed first, figuring Jack would think she'd never look there. When she saw nothing but a discarded T-shirt and her other tennis shoe, she decided to check the dresser. If she then turned up empty-handed, she'd try the shed outside.

Giving the banana another nibble, she put it down and opened his top drawer. After a few light pats, her hand struck something hard. Pay dirt.

Careful not to disturb the piles, she lifted the case out and opened the lid, exposing a jumble of tapes. She immediately guessed that Jack had dropped it. He must have been running late, because he'd never willingly leave anything of his in such disarray.

She returned to the end table and got Jack's tape, then dropped it inside the case. She would leave the microrecorder where she'd found it, because Jack would undoubtedly remember leaving it there.

This was like having another source, she told herself. While Jack worked, she would listen to his tapes. As long as he didn't know she knew who he was, he'd have no reason to suspect her. That wasn't the same as pumping him for information—at least not exactly. Actually, this turn of events was quite lucky.

Repeating this to herself, she got the bugs she planned to plant in the show saddles, stuck them in a pocket, then picked up the half-eaten banana. She had no time for lunch now, so it was all she'd have until dinner.

Yes, very lucky, she repeated to herself as she locked the door behind her. But as she passed a trash receptacle on the way to the stables, she dropped the banana inside. For some reason, her stomach rolled so badly, she couldn't finish it.

Cissy clutched Jack's note inside a hand shoved deep into the pocket of her wool jacket. A threatening storm had turned the air chilly, but that wasn't what made her shiver.

How was she going to act? *Love, Jack,* he'd signed. *Love,* Jack. During her afternoon of raking up the perennial horse droppings, she'd had plenty of time to think about Jack's deception. He was a cad, to be sure. But what did that make her? A caddess? After all, she'd deceived him, too. And would continue to do so.

So how was she going to act?

She crossed the patio and waved at some co-workers, then went through the great room to the kitchen.

Chaos reigned. People rushed out with food trays. Others rushed in, bringing back dirty dishes and containers. A cook yelled at an underling. She found Jack in a corner, putting steam trays on a cart. He looked up when she approached, and his face burst into a radiant smile.

"I'll be with you in a minute." Jack swiftly loaded the trays, then rushed past Cissy. "All hell broke loose. Someone let the lasagna burn and we had to fix a new entrée."

He dashed out the service door, pushing the cart in front of him. Cissy stood around awkwardly, and one of the other cooks gave her a suspicious glance. "Only help's supposed to be in the kitchen," he growled.

Cissy nodded compliantly. She wasn't up to eating alone with Jack anyway.

As she started backing out of the kitchen, a maid stepped out of an elevator, pulling a cart brimming with dirty dishes. Turning slowly, as if leaving the area, Cissy kept an eye on the maid. The woman took the cart to the dishwashing area, then returned to the elevator for a key still in the lock above the buttons.

After pulling it out, she hung it on a hook near the grill.

Unaware that an elevator existed, Cissy had despaired of ever getting to the upper floor until this moment. She'd tried the staircase once, but Bonnie had caught her and delivered a stern warning about the area being off-limits.

Cissy tucked the information away for later. Getting through the kitchen undetected wouldn't be an easy job, nor did it make her feel any better to know she'd used Jack's position for her own gain. Noticing the grumpy cook staring at her again, she headed for the service door and ran into Jack.

"Whew!" he said, wiping the back of his hand over his forehead. "The worst of it's over. I should be able to break for dinner pretty soon."

Shivering again, Cissy shook her head. "It's too crazy in there. You mind if I eat outside instead, then head back to the cabana early?"

"Sure." He looked disappointed, but then his face brightened. "Wait a second."

Pulling the cart behind him, he shouldered his way through the swinging doors and came back a few minutes later.

"Here." He shoved an éclair into Cissy's hand.

Cissy wanted to cry. What had gotten into Jack lately? She stared dumbly at his gift.

"I thought it was your favorite."

"It is." She bit her lip and forced herself to look up. "Thanks."

"Yeah."

A long silence hung in the air. Finally Jack broke it.

"I've been getting some flack about our different stories," he said. "What do you say we sit down and work out something reasonable?"

"I've been hearing the same stuff." But the idea of joining heads with Jack, planning a past that didn't exist... Another shiver shook her body. "You think of something. Let me know what you come up with."

She could see Jack's eyes dim, even in the muted light outside the kitchen.

"Sure," he said.

"Jack..." Cissy reached out her hand, but Jack was already turning to go inside.

"It's okay, Cissy," he said, an edge of bitterness in his voice. "Go on home. I can do it without you."

He then entered the kitchen, leaving Cissy to stare at the flapping door. She looked down at the éclair with a lump in her throat. For the first time since their arrival at the ranch, they'd reached a truce. But why now, of all times? It only made her job harder.

"You want to eat?" shouted a man behind the service table.

"What do you have?" she responded with forced heartiness, walking toward the head of the table.

"Whatever you want, Shorty," the man replied.

With this reminder of why she had to succeed no matter what it cost her, Cissy loaded a plate. But later, back in the cabana, she climbed under the covers and cried herself to sleep.

She awoke when Jack came in and she pretended to be sleeping. Soon the sound of his regular breathing told her he'd nodded off. She opened her eyes then, and stared at the pebbled ceiling, remembering how she'd barely been able to eat the chocolate éclair.

It was, she knew, the last gift Jack would probably ever give her.

10

―►◄―

What's bugging Cissy? Jack hung his vest on a peg in the employee's closet, took down an apron in preparation for beginning his lunch shift and continued pondering the question. She'd worked hard that day, he knew. And he had to hand it to her, she'd been up and out before he'd awakened, although the bruise on her hip must still hurt like crazy. No wonder she'd wanted to go straight home. But even though he'd ordered himself not to take it personally, her indifference the previous night still stung.

As Jack tied his apron behind his waist, he continued his efforts to blow off his injured feelings and was marginally succeeding when he saw Bonnie Katchum coming toward him.

"Jack!" Her hearty voice triggered Jack's well-developed internal alarm. What did she want?

"Jack," she said again. "I need a favor. Dave's been complaining that the kitchen is closed at night."

"Isn't midnight late enough?"

"Yeah, but, you see, Dave's a night owl. Sometimes he likes a late snack. So we've decided to keep the kitchen open twenty-four hours. Would you mind...?"

Jack wanted to cheer, but displayed the expected reluctance. "Well, Cissy'll be left all alone, and—"

"Jack." Bonnie's tone indicated what Jack had known all along. It wasn't a request.

"All right," he said with feigned grimness.

"Good. You start tonight. Go home now and come back at midnight. Your shifts will end after breakfast from now on." With a perfunctory thank-you she left the kitchen.

Only then did Jack let his exultant smile emerge. Dave Jordon? Late at night? Possibly half-drunk and talkative? Who could ask for a better break?

"What are you smiling about?" questioned one of his co-workers. "Thinking about going home to that pretty wife of yours?"

"What else?" Jack answered. "What else?"

What else indeed?

Jack saw Cissy enter the patio for lunch and waved to her. Apparently she didn't see him, because she went directly to the food line. Funny, though, he would have sworn her eyes swept over him. Suddenly he felt like the same gawky schoolboy who'd been rejected by the cheerleader, and amid a rush of inse-curities he thought he no longer possessed, he ap-proached Cissy in the line.

She looked over at him. "Oh, it's you," she said, in the same disdainful tone a prom queen might use with the class geek.

"Please," Jack said drolly. "Don't make a fuss."

"What are you doing here anyway? It's lunch-time." An expression of alarm crossed her face and her voice dropped to a whisper. "You didn't get fired, did you?"

"No," Jack replied with controlled evenness. "As of today, I'm working night shift."

"You are?" He saw she tried to stop it, but Cissy's face lit up nonetheless, and he felt a sudden prick.

"Don't look so miserable, Cissy," he said, resorting to the only defense he knew.

"Sorry." The line began moving and she looked away, making a big production of gathering her plate and cutlery. "I'm looking forward to some privacy, that's all." Her soft voice was lost in the noisy line to all but him. "We're always in each other's laps."

"Not really." He, too, spoke quietly. "Otherwise, I'd be having more fun."

"Stop it, Jack." She stared at him with melting brown eyes. "You're mad about last night, aren't you?" When he didn't answer, she went on. "I'm sorry I ran out on you, but I ached all over."

"I figured." But why did his voice sound so gruff? Her admission only confirmed that her behavior had nothing to do with him. Even today she was probably bravely bearing up under tremendous pain.

Feeling better, and because he'd already eaten, Jack stepped from the line while Cissy was being served, falling in behind when she headed for a bench. She remained aloof even when he sat beside her and immediately engaged in a conversation with a woman across from her. Jack was in the process of reconsidering his opinion of her behavior, when he heard a woman's voice purr behind him. He caught a glimpse of Bonnie, but knew the voice wasn't hers.

"Oooh, who is this cutie pie?" He turned to see a tall, brunette knockout. Caro Sloan. He'd recognize her anywhere. But why was she looking at him like that?

When Bonnie introduced him, he received his answer. With a feline smile, she held his hand overlong, then reached up and stroked his shoulder. "Look at all those divine muscles," she commented to Bonnie.

So far she hadn't bothered to actually talk to *him*, but just in case, Jack reached out and pulled Cissy into the crook of his shoulder. "I'd like you to meet my wife." He lifted Cissy's left hand, deliberately flashing the diamond. "This is Cissy."

"Wife?" Caro's slanted amber eyes narrowed. Jack could almost imagine whiskers twitching below her lower lashes. "I thought she'd be working. Oh, well...." She assumed a friendly smile. "Nice to meet you, Cissy."

He felt Cissy squirm beneath his arm in the wake of Caro's obvious insincerity, and she forced out an equally insincere reply. Or so it sounded to him.

The now de rigueur hush fell over the dinner crowd, and Jack knew Faraday had made an appearance. Caro lifted her head and looked above their heads to the spot from which Faraday watched her like the bird whose name he bore.

"My dearly beloved calls," she said sardonically, the velvet gone from her voice. She fixed Jack with a smile, her capped teeth gleaming white against her lipstick. "How does the line go, Jack?" With a wink, she drew her long crimson fingernails down his arm, lingering when they touched bare flesh. "Come up and see me sometime?"

She then floated away as if she were gracing a runway, leaving Jack with the impression that he'd just been part of a show that Caro had produced for her fiancé's benefit.

Slipping out of Jack's bear hug, Cissy turned and watched Caro walk away, feeling both irked and amused. The worm had turned and now Jack was the pursued. Not that he appeared as put off by the intended bride's attentions as she had been by Caro's betrothed's. In fact, while he hadn't exactly preened under the model's touch, he came damn close to it.

Caro was every bit as stunning in person as she appeared on the printed pages, and her scarlet halter-top catsuit accentuated every curve of her pencil-thin model's body. She moved with a cat's grace, too, which made Cissy feel thick and cloddy. Moreover, she didn't appreciate the way the woman had manhandled Jack.

After all, Jack had introduced her as his wife. Caro should have shown respect, although given Hawke's lack of the same, Cissy should have seen this one coming.

A wrangler across the table let out a muffled laugh. "Better lock up that man of yours, Cissy, before Caro lassos him."

Cissy laughed uncomfortably and was spared the necessity of responding because one of the other men spoke up. "That tempting tidbit's sure got her eye on him. Wish it was me."

"Yeah, Jack, the tidbit's got her eye on you." Cissy imitated Caro's feline purr, unable to resist this chance to pay Jack back for all his teasing.

"Cut it out, Cissy!" Cissy's head swiveled in shock. She'd seen Jack's indifference, his sarcasm, even his annoyance, but this was the first time she'd seen him snap in anger.

Her satisfied smile faded. The men ceased bantering. A pall fell over the table. Cissy lifted an eyebrow and Jack shrugged. She decided to let it go. She wasn't sure she could continue acting the saintly wife after what she'd learned about Jack, and if he strayed a little with a gorgeous model, well, that just made her job easier. Which was the first time it even occurred to her that Jack might take Caro up on her offer. Ignoring the pang that thought created, she explored it further. She could act the aggrieved wife then, providing reason to avoid Jack, at least in their co-workers' eyes. Still, she could hardly fool Jack with an injured act.

Unless she pretended he was embarrassing her. After all, even a make-believe wife wouldn't want to be openly betrayed. A perfect solution. So why wasn't she happy?

She gazed morosely into the distance, puzzling it out, and caught a hand waving above the heads of the other diners. Hawke Faraday was trying to get her attention. Aware that she'd spied him, he called out, "Hi, honey."

Cissy waved back unenthusiastically. It was Jack's turn to raise an eyebrow, but that gave no excuse for what he did next. He leaned toward her and captured her chin. Brushing his lips to hers, he whispered, "We've got to act like real newlyweds, Cissy. Academy Award-style. It's our only way out."

Her world spun, slowly, deliciously, until it contained only herself—and Jack. She wanted to open for him, deepen the kiss and let it take her where it would.

Act? This didn't feel like acting.

Yet, she realized with sickening clarity, that's exactly what it was to Jack. And he was obviously better at it than she was.

"Not *our* way out," she whispered back. "*Yours. I* can take care of myself."

"Hey, lovebirds!" Jack and Cissy sprang apart. Cissy turned to see Hawke striding toward them, smiling and wearing his irritating air of entitlement. "None of that around here."

Now standing before them, Hawke lifted Cissy's hand and placed his lips on it, lightly grazing the top of her diamond. He lifted his eyes toward Jack. "I lust after your wife. You're a lucky man."

Jack clenched his teeth and flexed his fingers, fighting the urge to form them into fists, and forced a lazy smile. "I'm lucky because she's my wife?" he drawled. "Or because you lust after her?"

Someone at the table gasped softly. Hawke's smile disappeared.

"Both," he replied, the tone of his voice turning hard. "Both."

He lifted his lips from Cissy's hand and she took the opportunity to pull from his grasp. She then glared at Jack, mouthing, "Don't."

Meanwhile, Hawke's eyes bored into him and he knew he was about to cross a line. In that moment he forgot his purpose for holding his backbreaking job, forgot Hawke was his employer and his key to success. All he knew was he despised the disgusting way the man pawed Cissy. Even more, he hated that she stoically endured it.

On the verge of telling Hawke to back off, he felt an object land in his lap. He jumped in shock as cold, sticky liquid seeped through his jeans.

"Oh, Lord! Look what I've done. Oh dear, oh dear, oh dear." Cissy's voice dripped with regret as she snatched back her lemonade glass. "Jeez, it just kinda slipped from my hands. Here, let me help." Picking up a napkin, she began dabbing at his soaked jeans.

Her fingers fluttered around his thighs, around the V of his legs, dabbing and moving, dabbing and moving, repeatedly brushing across his male equipment. He felt a stir, a tug.

"Oh, it's so sticky!" Cissy proclaimed. Dimly, Jack grew aware of grinning faces.

Good God! His mind filled with scrambled images. Hawke challenging him. His retort. Cissy's touch. Hawke glaring. His reaction. Cissy's touch. His growing arousal. Cissy's touch.

Suddenly Cissy jerked her hand away, and her eyes grew shocked and angry. Jack's jumbled thoughts snapped into coherence. In that instant he realized Cissy had spilled her drink purposely. He glared back at her, then fixed his gaze on Hawke.

His employer returned the stare. "Like I said, Jack.

You're a lucky man." With that, Hawke turned and walked away.

"Oooh, a ménage à quatre," quipped Terry naughtily. Cissy shot her a crushing look. So did her husband, and Terry had the grace to look away.

"Come on, Jack." Cissy climbed to her feet, waving her napkin at him. "Let's get you cleaned up."

Jack considered refusing, but circumstances made that unwise. Already regretting his confrontation with Hawke, he supposed he should be glad Cissy had intervened.

But he wasn't. In fact, he was damned ticked off. Cissy clearly thought she could handle Hawke herself, but Jack knew better. The man was a world-class lech who couldn't conceive of a woman not wanting him. Cissy needed his protection. Why couldn't she see that?

"She wants to take your clothes off, Jack," one of the wranglers gibed. "Don't fight it."

"Not funny," Cissy snapped, still yanking on Jack's arm. Resigning himself, Jack surrendered to Cissy's tugs, got up and followed her into the great room, which was empty, since people seldom had time to use it during lunch hours.

As soon as they were out of sight, Cissy flew at him. The napkin came flapping forward like a whip, nipping his arms and shoulders. She then lunged, grabbed each side of his leather vest and pulled mightily. Still in shock, Jack lurched forward. After his initial surprise, he planted his feet and found himself growing amused.

He felt like a Great Dane being terrorized by a pint-size poodle. Stained napkin still clutched in one hand, Cissy yanked and shoved, clearly trying to shake his brains out. Inexplicably, he hardened again.

"Don't *ever* do that again!" she stormed.

"Do what?" Not a purely rhetorical question. Exactly which event had so enraged her?

"You know what! Protect me from Hawke!" She punctuated each word with another yank. "You almost cost us our jobs! What were you thinking?"

With every shake, Jack felt himself strain at the buttons of his jeans. A smoldering ache filled his belly. He longed to reach out, grab Cissy's adorable buns and press her against him. Hard. Ease his ache, ignite a matching ache in her. Real hard.

It would be so easy to succumb. Her passions were aroused. The wrong ones to be sure. But he knew women. That passion could easily be diverted with the right move, the right timing.

And that's why she's a lamb being led to slaughter, where Hawke is concerned.

Wriggling to ease his growing discomfort, Jack caught Cissy's hands and pressed them to his chest. He tried to speak gently, but his words came out thick with need.

"You're wrong, Cissy. You're no match for Hawke. He's going to chop you up and eat you alive."

"You think," Cissy replied bitterly, fed up to the brim with Jack's lack of confidence. "You just think. But you know nothing about me, Jack. Nothing at all." She attempted to pull her hands away, but Jack held fast.

"Maybe not, but I do know men like Faraday. Hawke isn't only a name for him, it's a philosophy of life."

"Oh, isn't that poetic. Sounds like a song lyric." But left with nothing to yank on, Cissy felt her anger fading. Now she could see the genuine concern in Jack's eyes. And what was that huskiness in his voice?

Desire?

Concern, desire. A nearly irresistible combination. But she'd been down the road before, and while she sometimes missed Ed, her greatest regret was turning down that overseas assignment while under the spell of those twin emotions.

Well, dammit, not this time. She wrenched her hands from Jack's grip, lost her balance in the process and stumbled against him. His steadying arms held her upright.

For just a moment she leaned into his embrace. It felt sweet, oh so sweet. His chin grazed the top of her head, his breath stirred her hair. He smelled of the forest, of leather. She could hear the faint thrum of his heart, feel the steely muscles of his chest and thighs, feel how hard he was, how much he desired—

"Dammit!" She whirled from his hold, shocked, outraged and—oh, God, how could this happen?— turned on. "Don't ever do *that* again, either!"

To Jack's credit, he didn't ask what she meant. Instead, he followed the direction of her gaze, making Cissy instantly aware that she'd been staring at him with fascination. Her cheeks blazed.

"I'm a man, Cissy. This is what men do sometimes."

She hissed in a breath of air. "Well, do it somewhere else, mister."

With that, she spun on her heels and headed for the great room door. Before she passed through, she turned and threw the lemonade-soaked napkin at him. "And clean up that mess yourself. It wouldn't have happened if you'd stayed out of my way."

Jack caught the napkin with a swoop of his arm, then stormed after Cissy. He caught up with her at the door and grabbed her arm, pulling her to a screeching halt.

"Get this straight, Tinker Bell." His voice was harsh. "If you want to be my wife, act like one. And that doesn't include flirting with Hawke Faraday. You don't like my protection? Fine! But when you get yourself in trouble, don't come running to me."

"Look who's talking!" Cissy countered, aware her tone was rapidly approaching stridency and not giving one whit. "What about you and Miss *Caro* with her perfect acrylic nails? I half expected you to beg for a scratch behind the ears. Besides, who asked for your protection? What part of 'I can take care of myself' don't you understand?"

She braced herself for Jack's reply, but none came. Instead, he gaped in horror at the open French doors. Cissy's stomach clutched and she turned slowly, dreading what she knew awaited.

All their co-workers were staring at them. Off to one side stood Hawke Faraday. He was grinning madly.

11

When Cissy went to lunch on Saturday, excitement reigned. Faraday and guests were going to Los Angeles for a much ballyhooed movie premiere over Memorial Day weekend, and the staff would get a badly needed break. Most of them would have to work at least one shift, but otherwise their time was free. Cissy showed up in the middle of these discussions and one of the women asked, "Are you and Jack going into Reno that weekend?"

Cissy mumbled something about not being sure; another woman gave the questioner a warning glance. Suddenly everyone acted as if she were invisible. The same thing had happened the previous two days.

She'd eaten quickly, then headed for the cavernous great room and, for the third day in a row, searched the racks for a copy of *Movers & Shakers*. Again coming up empty-handed, she sighed heavily and moved to another rack. She only vaguely remembered the magazine, and supposed it was fairly new to the market. But Faraday's racks held some of the most obscure periodicals she'd ever come across. Surely she'd find at least one issue of Jack's magazine. With little hope, she lifted a copy of the *Tractor Journal* and found what she was looking for underneath it.

"Aha!" But her delight soon turned to dismay. It was a recent issue—dated only the day before, in fact—and Caro Sloan's face was splashed across the cover. Peering at an inset in a lower corner, Cissy saw Caro's wedding gown; the drawing looked suspiciously like the one Mama had given Cissy. She was still fuming when she heard footsteps behind her. Shoving the magazine back behind the tractor periodical, she spun around.

"Find something interesting?" Jack asked, sounding like he didn't really want to know.

"Can't a woman wander off by herself once in a while?"

"Whoa...." Raising his hands, Jack leaned back in counterfeit alarm. "Who are you? What have you done with Cissy?"

"Oh, right! Like we've actually been speaking to each other the past three days." She forced a nonchalant pose. "So, to what do I owe this unexpected pleasure?"

"Nothing you'd care about." He headed for the door, then stopped and tossed the next comment over his shoulder. "Saul and Mama invited us over again."

"When?" Cissy struggled to conceal her interest.

"Oh, you *do* care."

"Frankly," Cissy said, through tight lips, "I don't feel like going anywhere with you until I hear an apology."

"Me apologize?" His eyebrow lifted.

"Just tell me, Jack."

"Tomorrow night, for dinner." He paused, then wryly added, "I think it's a plot to get us back together."

"I'm afraid they'll be disappointed, but tell Saul I'll be there anyway. Now let me browse in peace."

"Sure thing, Tinker Bell."

Cissy pivoted and gave Jack her back. His satisfied laugh rumbled in her ears, diminishing as he drew farther away. Brushing away her annoyance, she slipped the copy of *Movers & Shakers* from the rack, rolled it up tightly and tucked it into her waist pack, then turned to leave the great room.

Oh, God! Hawke Faraday was strutting in from the patio. Would these men never leave her alone?

"Well, honey, if this ain't a nice surprise." Hawke checked out the room. "Seems we're all alone. It's good we've found this time together, what with you dumping that husband of yours. Don't you agree?"

Leering, he moved closer, cutting off Cissy's exit. Unless, of course, she wanted to bolt past him, and that would hardly look worldly. But what to say?

Realizing it was time to test her new strategy, she pictured herself as Madonna or Cher or some such modern version of the 1940s heroine and assumed a self-possessed smile.

"Well," she said, with a flirtatious swing of her hips, "it's certainly not all bad. But I'm due back at the stables now." She glanced at her wristwatch, then looked back with feigned regret. "Some other time, maybe."

"You forget, honey, I'm the boss."

"Why, I could never forget that, Mr. Faraday."

"Hawke, honey. I'm the Hawke."

"You know what, uh...Hawke?" Cissy gave her upper lip a playful lick, really getting into her role. Hawke would soon get the idea she was a woman to be reckoned with.

He raised an eyebrow in question.

"I bet you don't even know my name."

"Sure I do. You're Cicily."

"Try again."

"CeeCee."

Cissy shook her head.

"What do I get if I guess correctly?" Hawke cupped his chin with one hand and eyed her with mock thoughtfulness.

Cissy laughed seductively. Oh, yes, he was getting the idea all right. "A handshake and a cigar."

"How about something better?" He reached out suddenly and whirled her under his arm. "We could dance the bedtime tango in a private place just upstairs."

Hawke's breath carried its usual whiff of gin, an odor that never pleased Cissy under the best of circumstances. Their faces were now centimeters apart and his skinny lips were softening as though he planned to kiss her any second. Cissy had the sinking feeling she'd overplayed her role. Slamming her teeth over the squeal of alarm that wanted to escape, she spun from his hold. He looked startled.

"You lose this round, Hawke. I never do the *bedtime tango*—" she forced herself to drawl out those words, even though they scalded her tongue "—with anyone who doesn't know my name."

Steeling herself not to look back, she sashayed toward the closest door, the one leading to the entry hall. Slowly. Under her own steam. Her own person. Completely in control. The consummate woman-to-be-reckoned-with.

But by the time she grabbed the doorjamb, her heart was skittering against her breasts. Shooting a quick glance over her shoulder, she saw Hawke unaccountably grinning, which sent her panic thermostat soaring higher. She swung into the hallway and jerked the door shut behind her. Without asking permission, her feet broke into a run.

She'd traveled only a few feet when she ran smack into Jack. "I told you, Cissy, you're out of your league."

His self-satisfied grin told her he'd watched the entire scene. She gave a haughty head toss that was actually designed to see if Hawke had followed her, but if Jack mistook it for disdain, so much the better. In fact, for good measure, she gave another toss, this time adding a defiant lift of her chin.

"I put Hawke off pretty well, if you ask me."

"Put him off?" Jack gave out a laugh. "Is that what you think? Well, Hawke thinks just the opposite. He figures you just handed him the price of admission."

"He does not! Why, I made it perfectly clear—"

"That if he learns your name you'll take him up on the 'bedtime tango.'"

"Oh dear God! That *is* what I did, isn't it?" Cissy's hand flew to her mouth. "Oh, Jack, what am I going to do?"

Jack smirked. "Beg my forgiveness."

"B-b-beg! *Beg?* I never *beg!* And if I did, why, you'd be the last person I'd beg to!" Her outrage mounted, her gestures grew wild. "I've seen how you'd handle this. If you have your way, we'll be sitting on the highway trying to thumb a ride back to Los Angeles."

As her ire ran down, she became aware of Jack's puzzled expression. She could almost hear clockworks spinning in his head.

"What?" she snapped, spending her last ounce of anger.

"Why is this job so important to you, Cissy?"

"Huh?"

"I hear the wranglers talking. You're good at what you do. You could work anywhere. So why do you put up with Hawke's moves?"

"It's, uh…well, it's hard finding work this time of year. *You* should know that. Besides, if I left, you'd lose your job, too."

"This isn't about me, Cissy, it's about you. Of which, I now realize, I know almost nothing."

"Stop it! I feel like I'm being interrogated. I like this job, okay? Well enough to—"

Suddenly Jack grabbed her shoulders and pushed her to a wall, pinning her with his muscular chest.

"Jack!" She shoved back with as much force as possible, given the poor leverage. "What are you doing?"

He leaned down and muffled her next words with

his mouth. "Shh," he whispered against her lips. "Hawke's watching."

She was between the proverbial rock and hard place, feeling the squeeze. Hawke obviously thought she was now free to do...well, whatever it was he had in mind, and she'd failed to dispel that notion. Jack was her only refuge. But dear Lord, she didn't know if she could withstand this.

His mouth, so wonderfully soft, so softly wonderful, barely skimmed hers, but the touch was unbearably tantalizing. It made her want more...and more. Like tasting a tiny dab of homemade ice cream, like...

It was a matter of survival. At least she'd tell herself that later. But now, just for now, she opened up to him. Like flowers reaching for the sun, her hands slithered around his neck. She deepened the kiss.

In that instant she no longer cared about his secret occupation or his controlling ways or their frequent quarrels. Not while his tongue stroked the inner side of her lower lip so erotically. Not while his scent filled her lungs and his breath carried heaven songs to her ears. Why had she ever resisted him?

None of it mattered. Not Hawke. Not the story. Nothing mattered but Jack. Just Jack. Here. Now.

"Looks like the lovebirds have made up."

At the sound of Hawke's gritty voice, Jack broke the kiss. He stared down at her with unfocused eyes, looking dazed, as if he, too, had forgotten about Hawke. Still clinging to Jack, Cissy reluctantly turned her head in the rock star's direction. He stared at her for a second, then smiled ruefully, shrugged and walked away.

"See, Cissy?" Jack said, once Hawke was out of earshot. "It's our only option."

His voice sounded ragged. Had he felt what she felt? It would be so easy to believe he had, but she wouldn't indulge in that luxury. Nevertheless, she couldn't quite douse the flames of joy consuming her as she snuggled against his chest. She wiggled closer still, acutely aware of Jack's irregular breathing. His arms tightened around her momentarily.

Then he let go and stepped back. Gently removing her hands from his neck, he looked down and smiled weakly. "So, Tinker Bell, are you ready to beg my forgiveness yet?"

Cissy's joy burst like a soap bubble on the air. Jack *had* been acting! Well, she could psych herself up, she could perform, too. She had no choice, she realized, not after that disastrous encounter with Hawke.

"Okay," she said coldly.

"Say it." He didn't even pretend to be kidding.

"I beg your forgiveness."

With a laugh that sounded a tad phony, Jack replied, "The attitude needs some adjusting, but it's a start."

"Yeah," Cissy shot back. "But not of something big."

12

That evening, Cissy went to dinner arm in arm with Jack. To her embarrassment, several of their co-workers applauded, and they all beamed with approval. Then things returned to normal. When she and Jack took their places at the table, they were again included in the conversations, which still centered around the Memorial Day holiday.

She'd lucked out and had all three days off, but Jack, she learned, was scheduled to cook brunch late Sunday morning, effectively splitting their weekend in half. He groaned loudly about this inconvenience, but Cissy was delighted. The ranch would be a ghost town on Sunday, giving her the perfect opportunity to explore the upstairs suites. She could sneak into the kitchen early, snoop around and be out before anyone was the wiser.

"I'm scheduled for Sunday, too," groused Tiny. Several other people echoed him. "Some of us are going into Reno Saturday to drown our sorrows. Would you guys like to tag along?"

Jack looked over at Cissy. It would look suspicious if she refused. She nodded, and they fell into making plans.

As the meal progressed, Jack surprised Cissy by being unusually attentive. When they first sat down, he arranged her napkin with a showy flourish, and he hadn't stopped there. He made sure she got rolls and butter before they were all gone, and he somehow produced another éclair.

What's more, he made no sarcastic comments. Cissy suspected it was all for their co-workers' benefit, but his attention still pleased her.

Later, while driving back to the cabana where Jack would drop Cissy before beginning his shift, he said, "We survived that, didn't we?"

"What?" Cissy asked with a teasing smile.

His mouth turned up, too. An odd moment passed while they got lost in each other's smiles. "Pretending to be happy," he finally said.

"Yeah, we did survive."

"Umm…you think it'll become a habit?"

"At least it should get easier." *If we don't forget we're only pretending.*

They fell into a silence broken only by the hum of the electric cart. Soon they arrived at the cabana, where Cissy deferred to Jack's schedule and gave him the bathroom. She waited awhile, but her clothes felt sticky from the humid weather and she couldn't wait to get them off.

Jack's shower was running, so she hurriedly began stripping. Just as she dropped her bra on a laundry pile, the bathroom door opened. Cissy squealed.

Jack stopped abruptly, and the towel draped over his bare shoulder flew to the floor. Cissy's bare breasts, high and firm and not too large or too small, stood out against her creamy tan. The skimpy piece of cloth covering her woman's place looked like it could be whipped off with a single flick of a wrist.

His mouth went dry. Unable to tear his eyes away, he drank her in. He knew he should turn around, but couldn't. She stared back, her huge eyes shimmering.

"Jack..." Cissy dove for her robe.

"I, uh, was out of after-shave." He turned his back like he should have done in the first place.

He heard the soft sounds of the robe sliding against her skin. The sweetly spicy potpourri she kept in her closet filled the room with its scent. A Cissy scent. Part tomboy. Part romantic. All woman.

"I'm decent now," she said in a hushed voice.

When he turned, she averted her eyes and asked, "You done in there?"

"Except for shaving. Do you need it long?"

She shook her head, then scurried over the bed. Shifting from foot to foot, Jack focused on the worn and colorless flooring. The awkwardness would soon be over, the moment would pass, normalcy would return. Or so he told himself.

Then Cissy swung her legs into his line of vision. Toned from years of riding horses, and smooth as a polished gem, they were the most perfect pair of legs he'd ever seen. When she stood up to squeeze past him, his control broke.

"Oh, hell." His words came out like a moan. Disregarding common sense, he pulled Cissy into his arms, tangled his hands in her hair and kissed her.

Not soft, not tentative like before. No, this was a ravenous, an almost-brutal kiss.

Cissy responded in kind. She nipped at his thrusting tongue and, allowing the folds of her robe to open, flattened her breasts and hands to Jack's chest. A sigh escaped on her breath.

The sigh nearly undid Jack. A shudder swept his body. Lifting her, he backed into the wall and leaned, pulling her close. Thus supported, he nudged his thigh onto the sweet V of her legs. She parted eagerly and he raised her until she straddled his leg.

She was trembling now, as was he. Clutching his shoulders, she broke the kiss and dropped her head in the hollow beside his neck. He cupped her bottom, smooth and naked excepted for the thin thong, and pushed her against his leg, then released. Pushed and released, pushed and released. Each time he pushed, her knee brushed his erection. The ache, the need, was almost too much.

Cissy thought she might die from bliss. Except she couldn't think at all. Deep within, in a low place, there coiled a smoldering heat, waiting to ignite. She thrust upward each time Jack pressed her buttocks, and a whimper of frustration left her throat each time he let go.

"Oh, God, Cissy. Dear God." His lips grazed her cheekbone, his breath kissed her skin. He moved lower, nibbled on her neck, then traced his tongue along the line of her jaw. "You taste like heaven."

Cissy moaned and tossed her head. "Jack...now."

He tightened his hold on her and slipped a hand

beneath her wispy panties. His fingers touched her center.

"Oh, oh, oh," she cried, tightening around his touch. She squirmed against him. Hard. Harder. She needed him, she wanted him.

"Please...oh, Jack..." She squeezed a hand between them, began fumbling for the buttons of his jeans. She felt the hard hungry length of him pressing against denim fabric and she scrambled to release it.

"Careful, Tinker Bell." His words came out on a raspy breath. "I want this to last."

Suddenly she loved that silly nickname, everything about it. She loved the feel of Jack's steely muscles, the solid need of him beneath her fumbling fingers, the soap-and-pine scent of him. She loved it all, loved everything.

Most of all she loved Jack.

You can't! cried a frightened part of her. But when the last button came loose, freeing Jack to enter her, she lifted her hips and took him in, all at once, without reservation, like welcoming home a beloved warrior, and didn't give the voice a single notice.

Only Jack's virile and violently thrusting body had any meaning at all. And when, shuddering with wanting, his teeth grazed her shoulder, she hoped he'd leave a mark. For in that moment, as she shattered into a trillion small shards, being Jack's woman was the only thing Cissy cared about.

Even though he was running late, Jack belted out an off-key rendition of "Long, Tall Sally" while he drove to work. Of course, he'd changed the name to

Cissy, though she was admittedly neither long nor tall. Still, he couldn't get her name from his mind. It echoed in there between the words of the song. Cissy. Cissy. There, he'd thought it again. Cissy.

His only other coherent thought was "Wow!" He laughed, glad he had no midnight co-workers. Somehow he couldn't picture anyone else willingly listening to an entire evening of "Wow, Cissy!"

When he entered the kitchen fifteen minutes late for his shift, Bonnie Katchum was waiting by the pantry door.

"You're late, Jack." Her face was grim. "Dave's here and wanting something to eat."

"I'll get right on it." This was the third time since Jack started working nights that Jordon had appeared for a meal, but he'd never shown up this early before. Two, three in the morning was more like it. Once, he even appeared around sunrise, making Jack wonder if the man ever slept.

Jack grabbed his apron and put it on over his vest. Bonnie scowled, but clearly there was little else for her to say unless she planned to ask where he'd been, and Jack figured one look at him provided the answer. So, giving her an ingratiating smile, he hurried off.

Despite his bad reputation, Jack found he liked Dave Jordon's style. The man was direct, to the point and always sober. Twice, he'd invited Jack to eat with him and, figuring Jordon was one of the bosses, Jack had accepted.

He breezed into the kitchen, tying his apron as he went, and found Dave sitting at the kitchen bar with his elbows on the counter and his head morosely in his hands. His tie, which Jack had never seen other than precisely knotted, hung loose around his open shirt collar. His eyes were bleary.

"Where've you been?" Dave asked in a sullen and slurry voice.

"With Cissy. We lost track of time. Sorry I held you up."

"Yeah. Heard you two made up." Dave grinned slyly. "Caro was awful disappointed."

Jack stood there a moment not quite knowing how to respond. When Dave said nothing more, he asked, "What's your poison?"

"Got any Jack Daniel's un'er there?" Dave hooked his thumb toward a locked cabinet.

"I'll check."

After going through a complicated procedure to get the cabinet key, Jack rummaged and, sure enough, found the liquor. He waved it at Dave.

"How do you like it?"

"On the rocks, skip the ice."

"Sure, but let me get you to sign this." He handed Jordon a clipboard holding a running inventory of the booze, and the man signed with a flourish. When Jack put the board away, he noticed that the signature was almost unreadable. He reached under his apron to his vest and turned on the recorder in its pocket.

What luck! He didn't know what had set Dave off—rumor had it that the man drank sparingly—but he'd already had a snootful. Chances like this didn't come along every day. He got out a thick lead-crystal glass, poured it to the brim and put it in front of Dave.

"Down the hatch." Jordon tilted back his head and

took a big gulp. He grimaced afterward, the hot liquid obviously burned his throat.

"Maybe you better take it easy, man." Jack had visions of Dave collapsing with alcohol poisoning. "How about I scramble you some eggs?"

"Eggs'd be good. Haven't eaten all day." Swaying unsteadily on his stool, Dave took a more genteel sip. The glass sloshed as he put it down, and his head drooped back down onto his hands.

After turning on the big built-in griddle, Jack headed for the refrigerator. "Fried or scrambled?" At Dave's puzzled expression, he added, "The eggs."

"Oh, yeah. Fried, easy over." He lifted his glass. "You gonna join me?"

"Yeah, sure, if you want."

"Good. You're the only one here who's nice to me, man, you know that? No one else gives a damn."

"Sure they do."

Jordon shook his head slowly back and forth. "Nuh-uh. Not Hawke. Not any of his band. Not Caro. Especially not Caro. Nope, 'specially not her." He paused. "She used to, you know." For a moment he looked proud. "Used to think I was hot stuff. Real hot stuff. Really, really hot."

Jack stared at Dave. Him and Caro Sloan? Hard to believe.

"Don't look like that, man. It's true."

"I believe you." What else could Jack say?

Opening a bag of frozen hash browns, Jack spilled a generous quantity onto the griddle. Dave silently nursed his whiskey while they sizzled. Breaking four eggs, Jack watched the whites begin to curl and he waited for Dave to continue. Shortly he turned the potatoes. Dave still hadn't spoken.

"Don't know why she's marrying that bastard when she could have a man who treats her right."

Jack looked up and saw utter misery in Dave's eyes. Would he feel like that if Cissy left him? Even the idea was unbearable. For a heartbeat he felt remorse over pumping Dave in his darkest hour. Then his magazine's overdue bills popped into his mind's eye, and he remembered he couldn't afford a luxury like sympathy.

"You seem like the kind of man who knows how to treat a woman," he said, turning the eggs. The toast popped up with a ponging sound.

"Right on, man. But it doesn't matter." Dave shook his head again and weaved dangerously on his perch. "When the sun comes up on Memorial Day, Caro's gonna marry Faraday. Nothin' I can do."

"Well, I'm sure she's making a big mistake."

"You said it."

This was definitely his day! First, he'd bedded the woman of his dreams and then he'd been handed this prime story over a crystal glass filled with Jack Daniel's. Wanting to cover his excitement with activity, he scooped up the eggs, slid them onto plates, added the hash browns, then made himself busy seasoning food and buttering toast. Dave's visits to the kitchen were informal, but Jack still customarily included garnish, and so he now arranged orange slices and a colorful splash of parsley around the food.

When he finally looked back up, he found Dave

sprawled on the counter in a pool of whiskey. The glass rolled back and forth near his hands.

Poor devil needed some peace. Jack went over and touched Dave's shoulder, called his name several times. Receiving no response, he braced his arm around Dave's back and lifted him to his feet.

"Huh?" Dave muttered.

"Come on. I'll help you to your room."

"Awful nice of you." Dave leaned heavily on Jack and they stumbled toward the service elevator—Lord knew they couldn't handle the stairs. Then Dave began mumbling. "You're a real fren', man, that's for sure. A real fren'. Wanna know the truth?" He stopped, lurched. Jack almost lost his balance. "You're the only fren' I got."

"Thanks," Jack said, feeling guilty as hell.

Sometimes he hated this business.

13

Cissy woke up around ten in the morning, snuggled under Jack's arm. Lying on his belly, face on the pillow, he looked boyish and defenseless. Cissy looked at him awhile before getting up.

She wandered over to the chair, sat down, wrapped her arms around her legs and stared at Jack again. He'd had a long night and would probably sleep until noon; then they'd have the whole day until they were due at Saul and Mama's.

How could she be deliriously happy and abjectly miserable at the same time? Dear heaven, how had this happened? Somehow, when she wasn't looking, she'd fallen in love with Jack. Why now? she wondered. Why him?

Her feelings for Jack ran immensely deeper than the ones she'd had for Ed, but the choice was the same. Jack...or her career. It wasn't fair, and it didn't look like it would get any better.

So far, the bugs at Saul and Mama's had given her nothing but grief. She hadn't taken into account that a television could voice-activate the bugs, forcing her to wade through hours of "Wheel of Fortune" and the like. The chore had cost her countless hours of sleep. Worse, the bedroom bug caught some rather intimate sounds and phrases, and even now Cissy's face burned when she thought of how she'd invaded that nice couple's privacy.

Well, she'd fix the television problem at dinner that night and reposition the bug under the bed at the same time. Then on Memorial weekend Sunday she'd slink into Caro's bedroom and hopefully find a gold mine of information.

But would she first confess all to Jack?

"Hey, Tinker Bell."

Cissy looked up. Jack was levered up on the bed, grinning at her. "What are you doing way over there?" He patted the empty spot beside him.

Cissy jumped up and leapt into Jack's waiting arms, her burst of joy eclipsing her agonizing indecision. Besides, she told herself, as she lifted her face for a good-morning kiss, come Memorial Day weekend she'd have her information. Then she'd tell Jack everything.

"Come in," welcomed Mama, taking Cissy's and Jack's hands and displaying obvious pleasure that they'd patched up their quarrel. "What have you been doing all day? You're both glowing."

Cissy blushed, at a loss for words, but Jack came up with the perfect answer. "Nothing you'd be interested in, Mama."

"Or should be," Saul interjected. "You two ready for another free-for-all Monopoly game?"

Cissy laughed. "Another licking you mean."

"You've got that right," Mama said. "But first,

dinner.'' She waved her hand toward the table that overflowed with platters of food.

As Cissy helped herself to a slice from a rack of lamb, Mama began speaking of a bridesmaid who hadn't been able to get into her ceremony dress. ''She had a fit.'' Mama chuckled, appearing to cherish the memory. ''She cursed the seamstress, cursed the seamstress's delivery man and declared the dress either shrank in transit or had been made too small. Miss Caro...well, she just smiled and told her friend to lay off cheesecake for a week and the dress would fit just fine.''

Mama's eyes suddenly bulged. ''That hushed her up,'' she mumbled, reaching for Cissy's glass. ''More wine?''

Cissy's glass was still over half-full.

''Uh, no thanks,'' she replied, trying to look guileless. So the wedding would be soon. This crumb of information sent her mind spinning. Were Hawke and Caro hiding their ceremony by making a big production over attending the movie premiere? And if that were true, she thought, taking a bite of biscuit, it meant she'd soon have the story. Then she noticed Mama looking at her with faint worry lines.

''Yum,'' she said. ''These buttermilk biscuits just melt in my mouth.''

Mama smiled. ''Would you like the recipe?''

Cissy nodded and the mood at the table returned to normal. When the meal neared conclusion, Mama started clearing platters, and Cissy took advantage of the temporary confusion to peel off the bug beneath the table. Later, while helping Mama clean up, she put it in the kitchen, far from the howling television.

When the last plate had been stashed in the dishwasher, and she and Mama were entering the living room, Cissy asked to use the bathroom.

"Jack beat you to it," said Saul, busy setting up the Monopoly board.

Barely able to keep her foot from tapping, Cissy relieved her impatience by helping Saul. She wanted to complete this chore quickly so she could get back to the pleasure of pretending to be Jack's wife.

What kind of husband would Jack make? she wondered, as she positioned the game cards in their rectangular boxes. Did he have a bass-booming stereo and tons of CDs that he'd scatter all over the place? Would he mow the lawn regularly? Did he want children? If so, how many? Not the baseball team he'd teased about during the first night on the ranch, she hoped.

As she reassured herself that Jack was too tidy and practical to have any of the faults she'd envisioned, he came back into the room, wearing a frown. Cissy passed him on her way to the bathroom and raised an eyebrow. Something wrong? He shook his head.

Taking him at his word, Cissy closed the bedroom door and turned on the bathroom light. She then hurried to the bed. Two overlong stays in the bedroom would raise suspicions.

Going to her knees, she took a penlight from her waist pack, turned it on and swept the beam under the bed. No bug, so she directed the light to the corners. Seconds passed quickly; her nerves began jangling.

She couldn't stay much longer. Maybe the bug had been knocked to another location. Maybe Mama had vacuumed it up, although if that were the case, it must have been recently because Cissy had listened to the tape just Thursday night.

She pursed her lips, let out a frustrated sigh, then headed back to the living room. She still had bugs in the kitchen and in the phone, and even if someone had found the one under the bed, she knew they couldn't connect it with her.

Later that night, as he and Cissy walked to their cabana, Jack rubbed his fingers over the metal shard in his pocket. It had been smooth and round when he'd found it, but he'd stepped on it like he would the insect it was named for.

Who else was after his story?

"You're lost in thought." Cissy stared at him with curiosity, the moon painting her face with silvery highlights and sculpting her lips into deep shadows, making them look more inviting than ever. "Anything you want to tell me?"

Jack shook his head and forced a smile. Actually, he wanted to tell her a lot. Like about the bug he'd found in the bedroom while he was checking on the one he'd planted himself. Like who he really was and why this story was so important to him.

Maybe this was the time. He'd planned to tell her anyway—during this very walk, in fact. But that was before. Now his already-shaky ability to trust was strained to the limit.

Could she be his rival for the story? She was, as far as he knew, the only other person with access to Mama and Saul's cottage.

But Cissy? No. She was too guileless and outspoken to hide something like that from him. So who?

He'd think about it later, he told himself, moving closer and dropping an arm around her shoulder. "Come here, Tinker Bell. I haven't had a chance to kiss you all night."

Her face lit up as she stretched for him and wrapped her arms around his neck. When he tasted those sweet lips, Jack wondered how he could ever doubt her. Someone else was after his story—no question about it.

But not Cissy. No, never Cissy.

Nonetheless, even as his tongue danced with hers, his more cautious side warned him to keep his true identity a secret. At least until he discovered who'd planted that damned bug.

"Mondays are going to be hard," Jack said, enclosing Cissy in his arms on the threshold of the cabana. "After spending last night with you, I want to do it every night."

"Mmm, me, too." Cissy reached up, kissed him, then gave him a gentle shove. "You'll be late. Go on before I chain you to the bed."

Laughing, Jack released her and started down the walk, the keys to the golf cart jingling in his hand.

As soon as the door closed, Cissy double-locked it

and dove for the recorder in the closet. Placing it on the bed, she programmed it to rewind to the last counter number.

In the meantime she pulled her poached copy of *Movers & Shakers* from one of her dresser drawers, sat down next to the recorder and started flipping through the pages.

The recorder started playing. Once again Cissy blushed—Saul and Mama were as randy as she and Jack. She reached out and pushed the fast-forward button until the sounds grew more coherent.

"For the life of me," Mama was saying, "I can't understand why Miss Caro wants to risk messing up that beautiful dress by riding a horse to the bridge when she could have you drive her out there."

Bridge? Cissy's ears perked up, the magazine on her lap forgotten. She pictured Saul and Mama sharing a pillow, Saul smoking one of his infrequent cigarettes and listening to his wife speak about her day.

"But will she listen to me?" Mama continued. "Uh-uh-uh. I swear, as the wedding gets closer, she gets more stubborn by the day."

"Maybe she and Hawke think it will be romantic," Saul offered.

"How romantic will it be if she tears that gorgeous gown? What if she gets burrs in her veil? Good heavens, what if that palomino throws her?"

"Miss Caro rides real good, honey. No reason for you to worry about that."

"Shows what you know, Saul Coolidge!" Cissy could almost see Mama sitting up in indignation. "Cissy's been giving me lessons, and I've learned a lot. Even experienced riders can't know what an un-familiar horse will do.''

"More about the bridge," Cissy urged out loud.

"Even a shadow can spook a horse." Mama's voice rose. "And the wedding's at dawn. When the sun comes over that stone it could scare those horses to death. One of them could take off and ruin the whole wedding. No, no, it's a fool's idea. I've got to talk her out of it."

"Baby, baby," Saul soothed. "You worry too much. Two Moon Bridge is a bea-utee-ful place and the weddin' will work out just fine. Besides, you can't be worrying 'bout everything. You'll make yourself crazy."

"I suppose you're right." This was said begrudg-ingly.

"Come here, love. Cuddle up and go to sleep."

Cissy heard the whisper of settling bedclothes and soon the tape grew silent except for Saul's soft snores, which were almost lost in the excited beat of her heart.

Finally, the wedding location! Caro and Hawke were going to ride from the ranch out to Two Moon Bridge.

Wherever that was.

She needed a map, but surely she could find at least one such shop in the Reno phone book. She jumped up for the Yellow Pages, and the forgotten magazine slid to the floor. Cissy found herself staring down into Caro Sloan's slanty-eyed stare.

She scowled at Caro's image, then picked up the magazine and began slowly flipping the pages, searching for the masthead. If she didn't find Jack's name there, she'd move to the story credits.

The first time she saw the name—Jack Cochran, publisher and editor in chief—it didn't register. She was hunting for a reporter named Cook, not an executive named Cochran.

A perusal of the story credits didn't produce a Jack Cook, either, so she returned to the masthead and a sudden trick of light washed out the last three letters of the surname. When the fact struck home, Cissy felt like a horse had just thrown her into a tree stump.

Jack was no raw reporter, no hungry stringer. He *owned* the magazine and probably had years of reporting experience. Her chances of getting the Faraday wedding story from under his nose were slim, but if she told him about herself, she would forfeit any chance.

She considered doing just that, but memories of all the times her family had sadly said, "You tried" came to mind. "Tried" and "failed"—that's what they'd meant.

No! She couldn't—wouldn't—quit!

She got up then, ignoring an ominous thickening in her throat, and went to the dresser. She stood there for a long time with her hands on the top drawer, but in the end she left Jack's tapes exactly where they were, untouched.

14

———◆———

"Hurry," Jack urged. The excited voices of their co-workers echoed up the sidewalk as Cissy fumbled with the latch of her waist pack.

"Okay, okay." Finally getting the latch to hold, she gathered a sweater and rushed toward Jack's waiting arms. With a whoop, he swung her through the door, locked it, then whisked her to the van.

Inside, people were crammed together, their voices crackling with anticipation. Working six days a week left little time for play, and they were all as eager as ship-bound sailors with shore leave.

Cissy's own excitement teetered across the edge of anxiety. The last week with Jack had been pure heaven—and pure hell. One minute she was caught in a whirlwind of bliss, the next minute she swirled in an eddy of indecision.

"Shall we get off at Boomtown?" Jack asked as the van began wheeling toward Reno.

Cissy shook her head. "It's too far from the city. I still have to shop for my niece's gift."

"Mind if I bow out?" He chucked her under the chin. "I'd like to find a poker game somewhere."

"No problem." She meant it, too. She'd lied to

Jack several times already and that fact weighed heavy on her mind. Thank heavens he'd eliminated the need to tell another.

The lying would soon be over; that was all that kept her going. If it wasn't already too late, she'd have what she needed by the holiday's end. Mama's slip-up indicated the wedding would be held that weekend. In fact, it could be taking place that very moment, possibly even as she planned to sneak through Hawke and Caro's room.

Her fluttering stomach led her to realize what would happen if she succeeded. Front-page news for sure, and because it would carry her byline, Jack would know she'd deceived him. Would he be furious? Would he forgive her? Would he turn his back and walk away? The answers were too vague and frightening to dwell upon.

"Hey, Cissy," called Tiny from the driver's seat. "How'd you manage to get the whole weekend off?"

Cissy shrugged, laughed. "Just lucky I guess."

"Yeah, you probably snuck in and erased your name from the work roster."

"Would have, if I'd thought of it."

"Well I, for one, think it's because Hawke has the hots for you," piped up Terry, who was squashed beside her colorless husband. "You really are lucky."

Cissy groaned. "I can do without that kind of luck, thank you."

Everyone laughed, and one of the wranglers made a joke about Hawke's womanizing. Another round of laugher. The ride continued, full of jokes and chuckles, until Tiny dropped them at a casino.

To hide her agenda, Cissy wandered with Jack through the beeping sea of glowing lights for a while, stopping now and then to play a slot machine. Jack applauded when she jumped up and down after one of her tries paid off thirty dollars. Cissy chose to quit while ahead and followed Jack to the poker room, where they hung around, watching the games. When a seat opened up at a table, Jack said he wanted to sit in.

"Go ahead," Cissy said. "I'll do my shopping."

After agreeing to meet him at one of the bars in a couple hours, Cissy headed for a phone and called a cab. Twenty minutes later she was flattening a rolled-up map on the counter of a shop. "Can you show me Two Moon Bridge?" she asked the owner.

The woman leaned over and scanned the map. "You planning on going there?"

Cissy nodded.

"Oh, you'll love it! It's a spectacular arch of exquisite amber-colored sandstone about ten stories high. Water eroded circles through it, oh, aeons ago. Two of them, and they're so perfect, they look machine-made. That's how it got its name. The Native Americans—" The woman stopped at a point south of Reno and tapped. "Here you go."

"Looks pretty close to the highway." Cissy peered at the gold-and-green topographical markings.

"That's misleading. Actually it's almost seven miles down this winding road." The owner traced the road with her finger. "Roads are mostly dirt—if you ask me, the county should do a better job taking care of them. Anyhow, like I said, the Native Americans called the arch Two Moon Bridge because of those holes…oh, nobody knows how long, so we've always—''

"Where's the Rockin' Hawke Ranch?"

"What?" The woman looked taken aback at first. "Oh, it's not on here. This is a public-lands map and it doesn't show private property, but—" she speared a spot about a quarter inch from the bridge "—the ranch would be about here, if it was on the map, that is."

Cissy's foot started tapping. "How do you get to the bridge from the ranch?"

"You don't. You have to go in from the highway." She suddenly looked up. "Are you staying on the Faraday place? Say, are you some movie star or singer or something?"

Cissy laughed nervously. "Uh, no, I'm nobody. I just heard the bridge was on their property, that's all."

"Everybody's somebody, dear." The woman laughed, too, with a shake of her head. "The bridge does border the ranch, true, but you can't get to it from there, least not by car. Here, let me give you directions in from the highway."

"I'd appreciate that." Cissy wrote notes on the map's border as the woman talked about mile markers, forks in the road and landmarks, but left out all the side comments about stunning aspen groves and restful little creeks. She then paid for her purchase, but it took another ten minutes of nonstop travelogues before a new customer entered and took the owner's attention.

Cissy ran outside, a little breathless. She'd used up nearly an hour completing her transaction and still had to buy a gift. Jack would certainly ask about it.

Reno didn't have a real downtown, just a collection of business areas here and there and Cissy hadn't a clue where to find a dress shop. She got into the cab—she had asked the cabbie to wait, and at a pretty penny, too, she thought, glancing at the meter—and asked to be taken to a shopping center within walking distance of the casino.

Nothing went right. Reno's streets were jammed with holiday traffic. The cab moved at a snail's pace. When she found the right store, she found it crammed with customers and had to elbow her way to every display. Finally she pulled a pretty nightgown off a rack and edged up to a register. Purchase in hand, she practically ran the ten blocks to the casino, then leaned against the wall, panting, until her breath returned to normal.

She'd been gone nearly three hours.

Jack sat at the darkened bar, nursing a beer, thinking about what he wanted to say to Cissy over dinner. How should he begin? ''I love you, Cissy'' would start things off right. Then maybe he'd lift that dainty hand of hers, kiss the sparkler gracing it and suggest they turn the rental agreement into a purchase.

Was that too subtle? Did he need a more direct approach? Getting on his knees was out of the question, and he could hardly present her with a ring. She already loved the one she had.

He frowned suddenly, realizing he was jumping the

gun. He couldn't propose now. Judas Priest, he hadn't even told Cissy his real name!

His thoughts drifted to the eavesdropping device he'd stumbled upon at the Coolidges. Somewhere on the Rockin' Hawke, he had a rival. If that person beat him to the story—or even captured it at the same time and dampened his newsstand sales—*Movers & Shakers* would slide right down the tubes.

What would he have to offer Cissy then? He'd be a failed publisher, a failed reporter, a *fail*ure. Before he could propose, he had to tell her what she was getting into. No way around it.

Well, Monday was D day, and he'd know what he had by noon. He'd talked with his staff on the pay phone by the pool, and they were standing by, ready to produce a special edition all about the Faraday wedding. When it hit the stands, he'd find a copy, take it straight to Cissy and reveal everything. Then, while she was still stunned from the news, he'd ask her to be his wife.

Jack smiled, contemplating the scenario. Cissy would gasp, maybe she'd cry, then she'd fall in his arms and accept. Yeah, the plan would work.

Taking a celebratory, if premature, sip of beer, Jack glanced down at his watch, something he'd done regularly for over half an hour. Where was Cissy? Should he be worried?

Dumb question. He already was. Despite her slapdash ways, Cissy had proven to be invariably punctual. But forty-five minutes of tardiness was a little soon to be calling the cops.

Just then, someone called his name. A man. Jack turned and looked behind him.

"Cochran! It *is* you!"

Jack's heart missed a dreadful beat. It was Kurt—oh, what was his last name? Sanders? Landers? He didn't care. What mattered was that the guy often worked for Jack as a stringer and he'd shown up at the worst possible time.

Jack stood up and briskly shook hands, trying to figure out how to get rid of him. He was reminded of the time he and Kendall ran into a former classmate while they'd been on an undercover assignment. How had they ditched that guy?

"How's it going at *Movers & Shakers?*" Kurt asked.

"Shakin'." Maybe he could tell Kurt there was a dollar machine paying off like crazy in the other room.

"Yeah? What're you doing in Reno?" At Jack's hesitation, he said, "Oh! Working on a story, huh? Say no more." Then, a hint of question in his voice, he went on. "Been a while since I heard from you, Jack. Let me buy you a beer. We can catch up on old times."

"Well…I'm expecting someone any minute."

"Just a quick one." Kurt settled on the stool next to Jack. "Draft," he called to the bartender, holding up two fingers and gesturing toward Jack. "And one of whatever this guy's having. Say, how're Kendall and Nicole?"

"Michelle," Jack corrected, as the bartender set down the beers. "We all parted ways a while back."

Kurt whistled. "No kidding."

"Yep, I run the magazine myself now."

He chose not to tell Kurt the circumstances. They weren't something he wanted blasted across the industry. It occurred to him then that Kurt might be his mysterious rival. After all, he was in Reno, and Jack knew him to be a ferocious newshound. But how could he have put the bug in the Coolidges' home. Bribery, maybe?

"You haven't thrown much work my way lately." Kurt finally delivered the accusation Jack had been expecting.

"I've used mostly backfill in the last few issues."

"I see."

A silence ensued, which Jack chose not to fill. He let his gaze wander around, searching for Cissy and hoping not to find her. What if he just got up and left? He could go to another bar, come back later with an excuse that he'd gotten confused about where they were supposed to meet. Deciding it was his best option, he reached across the bar for his change.

"Cissy Benton!" Kurt exclaimed. Forgetting the money, Jack snapped his head around. There she was, dashing across the casino floor, packages clutched under her arm. Kurt stared at her in obvious recognition.

"You know Cissy?"

"Sure. We covered some concerts for *Top of the Rock.*"

"You what?"

"Concerts, man. You know, Grateful Dead, Mötley Crue—like that. We even covered Sinatra together. Boy, was that—uh-oh." Kurt's voice dropped several apprehensive notches as Cissy stopped in her tracks and stared at them, wide-eyed.

"Come on over, Tinker Bell," Jack called out in a chilling tone. "I ran into one of your old friends."

"You get away with calling her that?" Kurt asked edgily, inadvertently revealing just how well he knew Cissy.

Jack saw Cissy take several deep breaths, then she approached them like she was marching to her grave.

"Hello, Kurt," she said. Her eyes were strangely shiny.

"Hi, Cissy." Kurt stood up.

"Tell me again how you two know each other." Jack split his icy gaze between them.

The freelancer glanced at his watch. "Like to, Jack, but I'm late for an appointment." With that he slapped some money on the bar and headed for a nearby escalator.

Cissy just stood there, holding her packages like a kid hanging on to a teddy bear.

Jack returned to nursing his beer, not wanting to acknowledge her transparent sorrow. He'd had more than his share of betrayal lately, and this one—well, this one hurt like hell.

"Tell me about Kurt." He could see her in the tinted mirror behind the bar, saw her chest heave in despair when she climbed on the vacated stool. The paper bags crackled as she settled in her seat.

"He's someone I've run into now and then," she said softly, as if begging Jack to believe her. "I don't know him well."

"Funny. He seems to know you very well."

"What did he tell you?"

A hot ball in Jack's midsection burst into flames, and he whirled toward Cissy. "You're just trying to find out what he said so you'll know how many lies you can get away with! You're after the wedding story, aren't you?"

"It's my...my big break...." Cissy's image in the mirror ducked its head and seemed far away. Distant and removed, which suited him fine. "I wanted to tell you, Jack. I just couldn't find a way."

Who was this woman he'd come to trust, to love? Just a reflection of who he wanted her to be? An illusion, like the woman in the mirror? Suddenly, as if by its own volition, his fist smashed down on the padded edge of the bar.

"You think I can overlook this deception, Cissy? Just turn my head and pretend it never happened?"

She stiffened visibly, her expressions rapidly changing from shock to bewilderment to pain and back again. Finally her jaw tightened and she leaned toward him, leaving mere inches between their noses.

"Who are you to talk about deception, Jack *Cochran?*" Her voice was steady and frigid. "You haven't even told me your real name."

"How...?" Jack's mind spun with a million questions.

"You remember dropping your cassette case a while back?"

Jack nodded. He'd spent a good part of the next day straightening it up.

"Well, you also left your tape recorder on the table.'' Her voice softened. ''Your magazine's name was inscribed on the back.''

''So you looked for a copy at the ranch?''

''Yes, and I saw your name on the masthead.'' She looked away, bit her lip. ''At first I didn't realize it was you, but then—''

The bartender appeared and asked Cissy if she wanted a drink. She ordered a beer. While the transaction took place, Jack tried to digest what he'd learned. His jumbled emotions settled down, his anger ebbed, taking his protection with it. All that remained was a deep bruise that he feared would ache forever.

''You've known all along. Somehow that's worse than if you hadn't.'' He heard the bruise surface in his voice. ''Why?''

''Why the story?'' She reached up to touch his face, then stopped. Her hand lingered in the air a moment before she returned it to her lap.

''No, why did you sleep with me?''

''I knew I shouldn't....'' She bit her lower lip again and moved her head from side to side. Then she squared her shoulders. ''Because...I love you.''

Jack clutched his stomach, feeling like Cissy had just punched him. The words were right, although he'd planned to say them first. But where was the music, the champagne, the lavish dinner?

Where was trust?

In a few short minutes, it had vanished along with the beer in his draft glass. He'd believed Cissy to be one thing and now knew her to be another. He rubbed his eyes—they burned like crazy—then pushed his empty glass to the inner edge of the bar.

"Think I'll play another hand of poker," he said, over the lump in his throat, knowing it was the quintessential non sequitur. He then got up and walked stiffly away, trying to ignore the afterimage of Cissy's shocked and hurt expression.

He'd been worried about *Movers & Shakers* folding, that he would lose Cissy if he had nothing to offer her. But never ever, not once, had he imagined he'd have to risk his magazine to *win* her.

Could he take that risk? Would he?

15

She should have told him. Should have told him. Should have. "But I didn't!" she whispered vehemently as she watched Jack walk away.

The bartender immediately appeared. "Another beer?"

"No thanks." She smiled weakly. "Just talking to myself. It's a bad habit."

"I do it myself," the man assured her, then moved on to another customer.

By then, Jack had disappeared. She considered going after him, possibly making a scene, dragging him from the poker table and giving him the same hell she was receiving from her mind. But she didn't have the heart for it.

She should have told him. She was going to, really she was, right after—

Right after she filed the story with Top of the Rock.

She never quite got around to figuring out what she'd do if Jack accidentally learned who she was. Almost from the start, she'd known they were rivals; she shouldn't have kept it from him.

She sighed heavily. Years. All those years spent waiting for this second opportunity were on the line.

She couldn't sacrifice them. Jack couldn't ask that of her.

He hadn't.

The realization hit her like a bucket of cold water, and brought up a wad of rage. Jack hadn't said anything, not even when she'd told him she loved him. Not a single, solitary word. He'd simply stared at her and said he was going to play poker.

Poker? At a time like this?

What a jerk! Well, two could play that game. If he could walk off like nothing happened, she could, too. She'd find Tiny, maybe even the wild Terry, and go into one of the lounges, dance her legs off, have the time of her life. She'd show Jack Cook Cochran, whatever his name was. She didn't need him. Pretty soon he'd realize she wasn't boasting when she said she could take care of herself.

"Have another Long Island Ice Tea," Terry urged Cissy, who'd just sat down after swing dancing with one of the wranglers. The small cocktail table was crammed with her rowdy co-workers and she wedged in closer, giggling.

"I probably shouldn't. I sort of inhaled the first one." She felt pleasantly light-headed, and the pain of Jack's discovery was becoming ever more distant.

Fanning her heated face with a cocktail napkin, she noticed Terry flirting with one of the cowboys. "By the way, where's your husband?" Even as the question escaped, she knew it sounded critical. Worse, it reminded her of Jack. Her good spirits evaporated.

"Playing keno." Terry grimaced. "Yours?"

"At a poker table." Suddenly that drink refill looked attractive. "Hey, where's the waitress? I've changed my mind."

Several dances later, Tiny approached the table with his wife. "One more round before the bus leaves," he announced. "I'm buying."

Cissy joined everyone in a cheer and sang lustily when they broke into a round of "For He's a Jolly Good Fellow," which was mercifully drowned out by the band.

"Where's Jack?" Tiny asked Cissy.

She wished people would stop inquiring about the rat. "I dunno. Try the poker room."

Cissy wondered why Tiny frowned. Couldn't Jack play poker if he wanted? Then the man's face broke into a friendly grin. He ordered and paid for the drinks, before going off to round up stragglers.

When Cissy's glass arrived, she attacked it. Why hadn't she ever noticed before how well liquor soothed the nerves?

When Jack entered the lounge, Cissy was wedged between two wranglers, hanging on to their shoulders and singing with the band. Her head wobbled as if her neck was made of rubber and a silly grin covered her face.

He hadn't arrived any too soon. When Tiny had approached him at the poker table, Jack thought his hushed warning was somewhat of an overreaction. In his experience, Cissy never had more than one or two drinks.

Well, she was plastered now. Rather cute with it,

too. Her head bobbed unsteadily in time with the music, and she tossed it back now and then, giggling when the wranglers stopped her from falling off her chair.

But her state of mind was risky. Liquor loosened the tongue. If her mood changed, she might blab about their jobs without considering who was listening. Hurrying to the table, he came to a stop behind her chair.

"Cissy." He touched her shoulder. The wranglers faded away, leaving Cissy to sway upon her chair. She tilted her head back dangerously and peered up at him.

"Jack." Her smile vanished, the light left her eyes and Jack felt suddenly sadder.

"Come on, we're going home." He lifted her from the chair.

"I kin stan' up by myself." She waved her arms to shoo him away, teetering right and left in the process. Jack steadied her, then moved to support her weight.

"You're going to have a hell of a headache in the morning," he warned, guiding her to the waiting van.

She smiled up at him. "Does this mean you still like me?" She raised her voice and called to their coworkers, "Hey, ev'ryone, Jack likes me!"

"Shh," Jack hissed in her ear, glad nobody paid attention. "You'll blow our covers."

Cissy slapped a hand over her mouth.

"Keep it there," he growled.

Cissy tittered, but to Jack's eternal gratitude, kept silent as he shoved her uncoordinated body into the van. He settled next to her and she collapsed against him.

"You are so...o...o cute," she said, depositing a kiss on his earlobe. "I just love this hair." She tugged the silver-tipped thong down his ponytail, then looked over at their amused companions. "Don't you love his hair, too?"

"Oh yes, lo...ve...it," one of the men crooned. The others laughed.

By then, she'd slipped off the thong and looped it about his neck. Practically in the lap of the adjacent passenger, she dragged Jack with her and kissed the tip of his nose.

"Cut it out, Cissy," he grumbled, his neck growing redder by the moment.

"Hey, Jack, are you nuts?" someone asked. "Your wife's tipsy and in the mood."

"Yeah, Jack," said Cissy. "Tipsy." She kissed his nose again. "In the mood."

Just then, the van turned a sharp corner and nearly propelled Cissy over Jack's body.

"Oops," she squeaked. Jack caught her before she went flying and tucked her back under his arm. "Will you behave?" he admonished in a low voice.

"Ooo-kay." She dropped her head on his shoulder. The van continued swaying as Tiny made several more turns and Jack held her, glad she'd finally stopped horsing around.

When the ride grew smoother, he asked, "You aren't feeling dizzy, are you?" But Cissy didn't respond and Jack dipped his chin to check on her. Looked like he'd be waiting a while for his answer.

Sweet Cissy Benton, independent woman, horse wrangler, undercover reporter, make-believe bride, was passed out and gently snoring on his shoulder.

He didn't know what he wanted most. To kill her, or to love her till death did them part. Maybe both.

Cissy opened her eyes and stared up at the ceiling of her bedroom. A passing vehicle was casting fleeting lights through the room and they reflected into her eyes like a million poisoned needles.

Oh, God, where was she and what had she done?

The question vanished as she became aware that someone was pulling on her jeans, and she glanced down her legs to find Jack standing between them. His back was to her and he was tugging on her pant legs like a mule pulling a heavy plow.

So much for the sweet disrobing by a lover, she thought, remembering her final comment in the van before the universe mysteriously faded.

"What're you doing?" she mumbled foggily. The movement of her jaw did painful things to her head, and she decided not to do it again.

"Oh." Jack looked over his shoulder. "You're awake."

She wanted to say something witty, but not badly enough to actually talk. Anyway, Jack didn't give her time.

"Good. You can put your pj's on yourself." He picked up her silk shorties from the dresser top and dangled them in front of her. "Think you can manage that?"

Deciding that this sarcastic remark was simply too

much, she sprang to a sitting position. Her stomach immediately went queasy, but she still managed to snatch the pajamas from Jack's hand. Hoping for a jaunty flounce, she instead lurched off the bed.

When had the floor started rolling like that? she wondered, as her stomach went into warning spasms. Abandoning all dignity, she clutched the pajamas to her midsection and dashed for the bathroom.

Afterward, she took a shower, brushed her teeth and climbed into the green silks, but still felt only marginally human as she went back to the bedroom.

Heaven had failed to answer her prayer that Jack would fall asleep before she returned. Having turned on a lamp, he was still wide-awake, sitting in one of the tattered chairs with an Alka-Seltzer packet in his hand.

"This will help." His voice was gentle as he stood up and entered the bathroom. She fell on the bed and pressed her face in a pillow, fighting back tears. Once again, Jack's kindness had killed her. Somehow it contained so much more bite than his sarcasm.

"Here." Jack tapped her shoulder. He opened the packet and dropped the tablets into a glass of water. The brew frothed with a hideous sound, and Cissy grimaced as she downed it.

"You sure this will help?" She put the drained glass into Jack's waiting hand.

"Trust me." He took the glass back to the bathroom, and Cissy slipped under the covers while he was gone. She didn't know what he had in mind, but if it had anything to do with talking about *Top of the*

Rock or *Movers & Shakers,* she wasn't up to it. She rolled over and pretended to fall asleep.

She could almost feel Jack's eyes on her when he came back in the room, but she didn't move. Soon she heard the sounds of his clothes coming off, the click of a doused lamp. When the bed sank, she supposed he wasn't so mad that he'd sleep on the floor. Maybe that was a good sign.

She was kidding herself, of course. She would never pull this one together. Jack had been angry enough when Kurt had exposed her, and she'd just added to it by making a fool of herself in the lounge. How would she ever face her co-workers again? How would she face Jack?

Jack's breathing soon settled down, but he tossed and turned restlessly. Although he lay as far away as the narrow bed permitted, he still bumped her shoulder occasionally.

Each touch was like a slashing knife blade. It had come to this. Stacked together like two lifeless boards, connected by their mutual lies, the inches between them stretching like miles. Cissy blinked back the tears she'd been fighting all night, but this time one escaped and trickled down the side of her face. Sniffling, she wiped it away.

"Cissy?"

"What?" She squelched a small leap of gladness.

"About what happened, back there in Reno...?"

The bed sagged as he turned over, creating a valley. Caught off guard, Cissy couldn't help but roll. The next thing she knew she was up against Jack. Her head brushed his chin, her breasts grazed his chest, their thighs pressed together.

She started to lever herself away, but Jack crushed her to his chest. His breath sounded labored and she could hear his heart pounding.

"I can't stand this," he groaned.

Not sure exactly what he was talking about, Cissy didn't answer. She stayed very still in his fierce embrace, the sound of rushing blood drumming in her ears. He lifted her chin then, and brushed his mouth across her lips.

"Sweet Cissy," he murmured, then deepened the kiss.

They couldn't make love! Not now, with things the way they were! The knowing of that didn't stop her. Breaking apart inside from wanting him so bad, she met his kiss passionately.

"Jack," she whispered into a brief space between their kisses, "I'm so sorry."

"Don't talk about it. Not now."

She sighed. She didn't want talk, either. She wanted to be held instead. Touched. Kissed.

Jack unbuttoned the top few buttons of her pajama top and slid the silk down her shoulders, stopping just above her elbows. With the remaining buttons still secured, her arms were trapped. She struggled weakly, trying to free them.

Jack held her still. "Let me give you pleasure."

He bent his head and scattered hot, sweet kisses down the valley of her breasts, his trailing hair tantalizing her nipples. A streak of quivering need shot like an arrow straight to her center. She arched and moaned and tried to reach for Jack. Her silken trap held her fast.

"Let me touch you," she whispered. "Please."

Her breath was coming harder now, and her body felt afire.

"Later." Jack gave a throaty laugh and moved his mouth down the center of her abdomen. He moved low, lower, lower still, until he reached the band of her pajama bottoms.

Grabbing it with his teeth, he pulled the bottom with him and he continued down her body. Cissy lifted her hips to let the garment slide, wanting Jack, wanting him to kiss her. Kiss her *there*. Oh, *there*.

"Yes, yes, please yes," she whimpered.

A sound, caught somewhere between a groan and a growl, escaped Jack's lips. He released her arms and yanked down her pajamas. Cissy opened for him.

At the first flicker of his tongue, she felt a pleasure so intense that light and color floated before her eyes. Every nerve, every fiber, every cell in her body sang in bliss. She buried her hands in Jack's lush, loose hair, and let her mind slip away until she was aware of nothing but her thrusting hips, her burning body, the ecstasy awaiting her.

Immersed in pure sensation, she perceived Jack's murmur not so much as sound, but as a vibration that hummed through her skin. Still, the meaning was crystal clear and her heart joined her body in exultation.

"I love you, Cissy. Only you."

16

Better let sleeping dogs lie. The cliché popped un-
bidden into Cissy's head as she snuggled against
Jack's shoulder. Ignoring the rule about mixing met-
aphors, she decided to bite the bullet.

"Jack," she said softly.

"Uh-oh." She saw he'd been awake all along, and
knew exactly what was on her mind.

"We can't put it off forever."

"Why not?" He blew out a heavy breath of air
along with the rhetorical question and reached for her
hand. "I sure wish we could. There's so much at
stake here and I don't know if we can survive it."

He turned her hand over and kissed the palm.

"Stop it, Jack. I can't concentrate."

"I was hoping for that." But he released her hand
anyway and rolled to his side. "Will you clear up
something that's been driving me crazy?"

"Uh-huh, if I can."

"I found a bug in the Coolidges' bedroom."

"So it was you!"

"Thank God there's not three of us running
around."

Cissy sighed. "It might be better if there were. We

could let them have the story and leave this all behind.''

''You would do that for me?''

''Since there isn't a third person, it's a moot point.'' Cissy rolled to sitting position. Was it too dangerous to speak her mind? But if she didn't, and sacrificed this dream for him, would she grow bitter in their old age?

''I've waited so long for this, Jack. It's my first big story.'' She looked over at him, loving him so much it hurt. Yet, was love enough? ''I may never get another chance. I'll be thirty next March, and—''

''You think time's running out.'' He readjusted his position in the bed. ''I thought women your age worried about biological clocks.''

''That's the point. If I don't get my career started now, I might not be established by the time I want a baby.''

''Would that be so bad?''

''It's just—oh, Jack, I have so much to prove.''

''To whom? I love you just as you are.''

How could she answer that? His love meant everything to her. So did the respect she'd been chasing all her life, and she'd never get it unless she did something spectacular. She lay back down and took Jack's hands. Their fingers intertwined.

''I love you,'' she said, tightening her grip.

''I love you, too.''

''Tell you what.'' Jack kissed her forehead. ''We can do this story with a dual byline in both magazines.''

''You'd give up your exclusive?''

''For an aggravating brown-eyed blonde who has a razor-sharp tongue and the cutest little buns I've ever seen?'' He smiled devilishly. ''You bet.''

Cissy nipped him playfully on the chin.

''See what I mean?''

She laughed, then disentangled one of her hands and lay on her back. ''Trouble is, my boss'll never go for it.''

''He won't? Isn't semiexclusive better than nothing?''

''Nothing?'' Cissy raised an eyebrow, not liking the connotation hidden in Jack's question. ''That isn't an issue.''

''I have ten years' experience. You're a rookie.'' He hesitated. ''Be realistic, Cissy. Do you really think you'll scoop me?''

Cissy yanked away her other hand and shot upright. ''Let me get this straight. You think I can't beat you to this story, right?''

''Uh, no, that's not what I think.''

''Yes you do! That's exactly what you think! You're just throwing me a bone.'' She shoved her fingers through her hair, frustrated, annoyed, enraged almost. One more person who thought she didn't have what it took. Not that this should surprise her. It had been Jack's modus operandi ever since they'd met.

''Cissy...'' Jack rolled up and tried to pull her into his arms. She pushed them away.

''Be honest for a change, Jack.''

''For a ch—you should talk!'' He shook his head, sending his dark sheet of hair flying around his shoulders. "Look, I'm willing to compromise, okay? If you don't want in, say so."

"That just proves it! You *don't* believe I can do it." She poked Jack's chest. "Well, we're even-steven now. I know who you are, you know who I am. So do your job, I'll do mine." She got up and started yanking on her pajamas. "I'm going to get this story to press before you even figure out what's going on. Count on it!"

The sounds coming from Jack's mouth puzzled her at first. Then, suddenly realizing it was laughter, her fury exploded.

"You're impossible, Jack Cook Cochran, whoever you are!" She snatched a blanket from the bed, then stomped to the easy chair and flopped down.

"Don't let those broken springs poke you in the fanny, Tinker Bell."

Fuming, Cissy curled up, wrapped herself in the blanket and gritted her teeth, listening to the rhythmic rocking of the bed. She'd heard him roll over and guessed he had buried his face in his pillow.

The rat was still laughing.

Still in a twilight sleep, Jack moved to gather up Cissy and found an empty bed. Shocked into remembrance, he sat up and looked over at the easy chair. Cissy's abandoned blanket hung over its back. Given her overindulgence the previous night, he'd expected her to sleep until noon.

He supposed she'd woken up with the granddaddy of all headaches, and since they used the last of the coffee the previous morning, she'd decided to get some from the main house.

He could use a cup himself. He wasn't due for another hour, but he decided to go straight to work. He'd put on a pot, maybe add in some pricey, flavored grounds and share a cup with Cissy before his day started.

She'd be spitting fire at him, of course, but he'd tease her out of it. After all, she was being totally unrealistic with her puffed-up insistence that she'd scoop him.

He snickered cynically, then got up and walked into the bathroom where he turned on the water. He'd been a little hard on her, he guessed. Laughing *had* been out of line.

He stepped under a too-cool shower and began scrubbing, suddenly feeling the need to hurry. Forgoing a shampoo, he turned off the faucets, began briskly toweling off and told himself that any *reasonable* person would know that beating him was a losing proposition. And as long as he was looking at this from both sides, where was her gratitude? His offer had been mighty generous. He needed this story to save his magazine, yet was willing to share it with the biggest publication in the industry, putting his own business right there on the firing line.

Cissy had no appreciation. In fact, she was the one who should apologize, and he'd keep that in mind as he brewed her coffee.

It was when he climbed into his jeans that he wondered when he'd developed this blind spot. Cissy didn't know he was going bankrupt. How could she? He'd never told her.

Well, he would now. He'd put on the brew, get out breakfast fixings for the hung-over crew and hunt for her. Then he'd tell her all about Michelle and Kendall and how much he needed the Faraday story. He'd explain he was doing this for both of them, that the magazine would belong to them jointly once they were married.

She'd see. She'd come around. Absolutely. But as Jack drove to the main house, he found himself wishing that the gnawing doubt in the corner of his mind would go away.

The brisk walk to the main house cleared the cobwebs from Cissy's mind and combined with her small case of jitters to bring her fully awake. She tiptoed into the kitchen prepared with a glib excuse in case she encountered someone. Relieved to find it empty, she headed straight for the key to the service elevator and slipped it off the hook.

By the time she entered the elevator, her jitters had turned to jangles, and when the door opened, she was a pure bundle of nerves. Peeking hesitantly into the empty hallway, she wondered where to find Caro's suite. She doubted the room would feature a nameplate.

Remembering that she'd once seen Caro turn into this hallway from the top of the curving staircase, Cissy took a chance and tiptoed in the same direction the model had taken. The prospect of setting a floorboard creaking or encountering a sudden opening door terrified her.

Thankfully, most of the doors were already open, and as she crept down the hall, she caught a glimpse of a four-foot shot of Caro's face. Either her room, or Hawke's, Cissy concluded. She went inside. The eclectic furnishings were clearly feminine, and judging by the blowups all over the walls, she was in Caro's sitting room all right.

White wicker furniture with cushions of a muted abstract print formed a conversation area in front of a stone fireplace. A dais ran across the other end of the room and was occupied by a sculpted art deco lounger over which floated a curvy silver lamp. Here, too, was a rolltop desk in pale satiny wood with a chair upholstered to match the lounger.

Cissy stepped onto the platform and rolled open the desk, revealing a chaotic stack of ledgers and papers. Fearing that anyone who could be *this* disorganized could easily fail to record her own wedding date, Cissy began riffling through anything that remotely resembled an appointment book. Just as she opened a leather-bound calendar, she heard a noise behind her.

17

S̲he clutched the luxurious leather book to her breast like a shield and pivoted slowly. In a doorway leading away from the seating area, stood Hawke Faraday, wearing nothing but a pair of skimpy neon-green briefs.

His hair jutted out in wild tufts as he ran his fingers through it and stared bemusedly at Cissy. His near-naked body, although toned from frequent workouts, still revealed his advancing years, and one side of his face was creased from his pillow.

Not a sight to grace the cover of *Top of the Rock,* Cissy thought giddily.

"Hawke!" What was he *doing* here? He was supposed to be in Los Angeles. She'd been hoping to say something more sophisticated, but his squealed name was all that escaped.

"Were you looking for me—" He paused, smiled appreciatively, then drawled "Cissy…?"

When she didn't answer, he came swaggering toward her, and the suggestion in his movements alarmed her immensely.

"Isn't that the magic word?"

"I'm sorry?" Something had glued her feet to the floor.

"Your name. That *is* your name, isn't it?"

"Uh, well…yes." What else could she say?

"Then it's time I collect on your promise."

"My, um, my promise? What promise would that be?"

"You know, honey, the bedtime tango." He stood in front of her now and reached out to draw a single finger along her cheek. "You little rascal, you must have seen us drive in last night."

"Oh, well, let me explain." She edged along the front of the desk, away from Hawke's caress, and forced a laugh. "I never dreamed you'd learn my name."

"You're worth it, honey." He sounded as if he expected her to swoon with gratitude over his enormous effort.

"I, uh, thought we might get to know each other. You know, talk, stuff like that."

"Talk?" He looked puzzled. "About what?"

"Oh, hopes, dreams, that kind of thing."

Hawke frowned like he thought she was nuts, which Cissy supposed seemed likely from his perspective. After all, once you became a world-class rock star, how much larger could your dreams get? Then he tossed his head and laughed.

"I'll show you dreams." He pulled her smack-dab against his bare chest.

"Hawke, please." She braced her hands against him and arched away.

"What're you doing in the Hawke's aerie, if you

don't want to mate?'' he groused. He glanced suspiciously at Caro's open desk. "That is why you came up, isn't it?''

Deciding innocence was her best weapon after all, Cissy widened her eyes. "It's too soon. We've barely—''

Hawke's mouth came heavily down on hers, and before she could struggle, he began carrying her to the rattan sofa, still grinding his lips into hers.

Jack found the elevator door open when he entered the kitchen and immediately knew where Cissy had gone.

Why, that little—

He couldn't help grinning. Seemed he'd underestimated her, after all, and might actually find himself scooped. Well, it was time to put a crimp in her plans. He got into the elevator, amusing himself on the trip up by envisioning the hand-caught-in-the-cookie-jar look on Cissy's face when he surprised her.

His smile vanished when he walked onto the upstairs floor and heard the distressed cries. Breaking into a run, he followed the sound.

"Stop! Stop! Stop it!'' he heard Cissy yell. He dashed into a room he thought her voice had come from, and saw a tangle of arms and legs flailing over the back of a sofa.

"Dammit, I said no!'' A fist he recognized as Cissy's came up, slammed down.

"Ouch! Wha'd you do that for?'' Hawke's yellow thatch of hair bobbed up.

"I told you to let me go!''

Jack roared. Diving for the sofa, he yanked Hawke up by his hair. "Get off her, you son of a bitch!"

"What the hell?"

The singer whirled to his feet, obviously stunned that anyone would dare manhandle his person. He weaved between each foot, clenching and unclenching his fists.

Cissy scrambled from the sofa. Tugging her fleece shirt down over her partially opened jeans, she darted to Jack's side. He cupped her chin with his hand. "You okay?"

She rubbed the back of her hand over her lips like she'd just tasted something despicable, and nodded.

"Get that tart out of here!" Hawke snarled. "And if you want to keep your jobs, keep her outta my face!"

Jack's fist shot out. With an alarmed cry, Cissy leapt to stop him, but he brushed her off. His knuckles slammed into Hawke's jaw with a nasty crunch that gave him enormous pleasure. The star's eyes rolled back. He wobbled to the sofa and collapsed in a heap.

"Oh God, Jack," Cissy cried. "Why did you do that? We'll get fired for sure. He'll never forgive us for *this!*"

Her eyes began darting around the room and she fell to her knees, frantically peering under the sofa, the love seat, the chair.

"What are you looking for?"

"Caro's appointment book." She got up and headed for the dais. "I know where the wedding will be. Now all I need is the date."

Jack followed, caught her hand and tugged. "Come

on, let's get out of here. You don't need the book. You know the location and I already have the date. That's all we need. We'll cover the wedding together."

"Sure we will," she snapped, jerking her hand away. "Oh, there it is."

Jack heard feet running down the hall and groaned. "I told you we should get out of here."

"Who cares?" Cissy zipped her jeans and shoved the date book into them. "You've already cost us our jobs."

"I was defending you!"

"Did I ask for your help?"

Dave Jordon exploded through the door like a ferocious mother bear defending her cubs. "What's going on here?"

Jack pointed at the sofa. "Hawke and I had a run-in."

Dave looked at his crumpled meal ticket and groaned. "He always did have a glass jaw, even in the old days." He glared over at Jack. "What the hell were you thinking?" Then his eyes stopped at Cissy's wild hair and whisker-scratched face. "Oh, I see."

Jack noticed that Cissy had the grace to blush, and was tempted to let Dave think she had been a willing participant. But only tempted. "I caught Hawke forcing himself on Cissy."

"Forcing himself? How did she get up here?"

Jack searched for a plausible explanation.

"Never mind. You two are history anyway. No one gets away with decking the boss."

Dave went to the wet bar and took an ice pack from

a small refrigerator. By then, Hawke was struggling to sit up, and with an angry groan he took the proffered pack from Dave's hand. Cautiously applying it to his jaw, he glanced at Jack.

"Hell of a punch, man." Then he looked back at Dave. "Get rid of them."

"No worries."

Dave escorted Jack and Cissy from the room. As they followed him, Jack saw Cissy grinning in triumph. When he lifted a questioning eyebrow, she patted the date book hidden under her bulky shirt. "Mine," she mouthed.

Why hadn't Jack just butted out? Cissy wailed to herself as she huddled in the back of the limousine that was taking them into Reno. As thick and arrogant as Hawke was, the man wasn't a rapist. After she'd pummeled him smartly on the back, he'd gotten the message. Or was it when she bit his lip? No matter, the point was, she'd had it under control.

Until Jack burst in like an avenging angel and ruined everything. Now people thought she'd sneaked upstairs to meet Hawke, that Jack had caught them flagrante delicto, thereafter decking Hawke and trying to cover up for her. Telling the truth was unthinkable, so Cissy was left marked with a scarlet letter. At least Saul wasn't driving today—he and Mama had gone to Los Angeles with the others. Cissy didn't think she could bear facing his disappointment.

But that would change when her story hit the newsstands. Everyone would know her real reason for being upstairs. They'd still think she was a sneak, of course, but they couldn't brand her a trollop.

At least she'd have that satisfaction. Jack was barely talking to her now. He'd nodded and grunted throughout their entire packing process and was even now staring morosely out the window, completely ignoring her. He shouldn't have treated her that way, she now thought. He'd made her mad. Really mad. But she'd gotten even.

Several hours had passed before it hit her that Hawke's presence on the ranch confirmed that the wedding had not yet taken place, but, as she had feared, Caro's calendar had not contained the date. So when Jack went to the shed for the rest of his things, she'd gone into his dresser drawer and found what she needed. Safe in the trunk, inside her suitcase, was the cassette he'd so scrupulously lettered with the words *Jordon, Interview, Wedding Date,* and the little plastic jacket in his black case now held a blank one.

Although she hadn't yet listened to the tape, she knew it contained all she needed.

She scrunched deeper into her corner of the limousine and cast a baleful glance at Jack, then patted the pack at her waist. She had an open dated airplane ticket and a company credit card in there. The Faraday wedding story was hers. She had it all worked out. She'd tell Jack she was staying in Reno a few days, rent a car and prepare for the big day.

Funny, though, with success almost in her grasp, how much she felt like crying.

Cissy sat on the bed in the Lazy Eight motel room, turning the unplayed cassette in her hand, lost in the reflections off its plastic case. Jack hadn't been fooled by her announcement that she wasn't flying out that day. With a dark penetrating stare, he told her he'd be staying over, too. She'd heard a warning in his tone.

Now she dismally considered the strange coincidence that had brought her to this point. Of all the men in the world, why had JoJo accidentally hitched her up with another reporter?

Her hand involuntarily clutched the cassette case and she let out a yelp when the corner stabbed her hand. The answer was right under her nose. Why hadn't she seen it before?

JoJo knew who they both were. He'd known all along, and put them together anyway. Why?

Slamming the cassette on the bedside table, she picked up the telephone and dialed. When JoJo answered, she skipped the preambles.

"Who is Jack Cochran?" she demanded to know.

"Cochran, Cochran," JoJo replied breezily. "Let me think, darling."

"JoJo!"

"Okay, I'll fess up. Remember the guy I've been trying to fix you up with?"

JoJo was always trying to fix her up with someone, so Cissy only vaguely remembered. "Was that Jack?"

"Bingo. 'Course he was tied up with some witch— nobody as good as you, darling—so he wasn't any more cooperative than you were." JoJo made a tsking sound. "But when you both called about the Faraday wedding on the same day, well, I have to tell you, the opportunity seemed sent from heaven."

"You shouldn't have done it, JoJo." She tried to stop it, but the heartbreak in her voice still came through.

"You two have a lover's quarrel?"

"Worse. It's over, and it never really even started."

"Work it out, Cissy," JoJo advised. "Love doesn't come along very often—believe me, darling, I know. You've got to be on the lookout for it and cherish it once it's found."

"At the cost of my career?" Cissy asked heatedly. "How can you say that?"

"Work, work, work." He sounded uncharacteristically impatient. "Life is more than work. You and Jack are alike, noses so buried in your jobs, you can't see all the good things life offers. When are you going to learn, Cissy, that the world won't end if you don't become a star reporter?"

"Yes, it will," she wailed. Ridiculous, of course, but every cell in her body believed it. "If I don't get this story, it'll just prove everybody was right."

"Are you in love with *everybody?* Or just Jack?"

Cissy grew suddenly mute and looked down at her balled hand. The solitaire winked up, as though it held a secret. She'd have to return the ring soon, give it back. Give Jack back. Her conflict grew unbearable.

JoJo's urgings grew even more so. From the day she'd met him on the Berkeley campus, he'd been her adviser, the only person who consistently believed in her abilities. She always listened to his advice, usually took it. But now? No, he asked too much.

"I can't talk anymore," she said in a thickening voice.

"Cissy..." But JoJo's protest faded into nothing as Cissy lowered the receiver to the hook.

She clutched her midsection and stared at the blank wall of her room, silent tears streaming down her face. At first, she didn't fight them, but after a while she sniffled, then leaned forward and picked up the tape.

Therein was contained her prize. She had only to put it in the cassette player and everything she'd dreamed of would be hers. But when she'd conceived that dream, Jack hadn't even been a gleam in her eye, and the dream had not, in any form, included trading the man she loved for fame and glory.

When the rap came, Jack had just put the Jordon tape in his player and was settling down to give it another listen. He now smothered his jolt of hope and got up to answer the door. If it were Cissy, and he fervently hoped it wasn't, well, he'd tell her to take a hike.

Faraday nearly raped her, for God's sake, yet she had the nerve to say I screwed up! There was a limit to what he could take.

He jerked open the door, banging it against the inside wall. Cissy gave a small jump and stared up at him from beneath spiked eyelashes. She smiled shyly. "Hi."

She looked small and fragile and infinitely delectable, all bundled up in that oversize fleece shirt. Her curls tumbled about her round chocolate eyes and Jack ached to crush her to his chest.

"You want something?" he asked curtly.

"To talk." She stepped forward. "Can I come in?"

"What's wrong?" he replied caustically, but he stepped aside to let her in anyway. "Did you fail to find that precious date in Caro's book?"

"Actually, yes. But that's not why I'm here."

"Sure it is," Jack responded, unwilling to listen to her lies. He hurt, deep within, in some secret and usually protected place.

"You mean more to me than the story." She rubbed her hands together, entwined her fingers, and held them in front of her. Looking directly in his eyes, she announced, "I love you, Jack."

Every muscle in Jack's body froze. Her words rang with sweetness. Oh, sweet, so sweet, and they sparked a longing so intense, it terrified him.

Terror took over and he lashed out. "Bull! Don't kid a kidder, Cissy. You've come to ask me when the wedding is."

"No." A shake sent her curls flying. "I'm here to tell you where the wedding's being held. I want *you* to have the story."

"In my dreams!" Jack spun away and walked to the window, gazing out on the paved parking lot below. Part of him wanted to believe, and he feared that part most of all. "Get out of here, Cissy. I'm tired of being used."

"U-u-used?" Her voice thickened, yet still he

didn't turn around. Silence filled the room, broken only by the slamming of a car door outside. When Cissy spoke again, it was with resignation. "I suppose you have a right to believe that."

"I asked you to go." He couldn't stand to hear any more lies.

He heard footsteps, the door opened. "The wedding's at Two Moo—"

"Out!" he shouted to the window.

He expected a slamming door, but heard only a soft click. Cissy was gone.

His body felt heavy, like an old man's, as he shuffled back to the cassette player. Everything he'd worked for, dreamed of, was at stake. He knew he'd cut his own throat by refusing to hear Cissy out, but he hadn't believed she was giving him the true location anyway. It was probably a ruse, meant to throw him off the track.

He pushed the play button on his recorder and sat down to listen. The muscles in his back screamed, his shoulders spasmed, and he flexed them to ease the tension, noticing that believing the worst of Cissy made him feel better. After he finished reviewing the tape, he'd think of every revolting, nasty thing she'd ever done. By the time he left Reno, he'd have the story in the bag and a million grievances against her.

Suddenly he realized he wasn't hearing any voices from the recorder. He pushed fast forward and encountered only static. A few more seconds passed before he found out the tape was blank.

A howl of rage burned through his throat and in that instant he knew he had still clung to a slim thread of hope. Now it snapped. He leapt for the door and ran down the hallway to Cissy's room.

He pounded on her door, yelling her name—"Cissy! Cissy! Cissy!"—and received no answer.

Other doors opened, voices murmured. Someone asked, "What's going on?"

Jack stopped midslam and saw several people staring at him with alarm. Struggling to control his rage, he mumbled. "Uh, she's a heavy sleeper. Sorry to disturb you."

He stumbled back to his own room then, his mind spinning. Where had Cissy gone? Had she left Reno? He laughed bitterly. With the time and location of the wedding in her pocket? Highly unlikely. But still he called the front desk and asked if Cissy had checked out.

"No," the woman replied. "Although she was here a little while ago, inquiring about rental cars."

After asking the woman to arrange a car for him, too, Jack hung up and reviewed his options. Never wondering why Cissy even bothered since she had the tape in her hot little hands, Jack congratulated himself in fending off her attempts to ferret the date from him.

He still had his hand on the telephone when it rang.

Cissy! She'd come to her senses.

Steeling himself to be gracious, yet aloof, he picked up the receiver.

"Jack," said JoJo's voice on the other end, smashing Jack's fragile fantasy. "Listen, darling, I've something to tell you."

18

A little after three the next morning, in a Jeep piled high with equipment, Cissy began the long trip in the direction of the Rockin' Hawke Ranch. She felt miserable, not at all the way she'd once imagined feeling with a plum story almost in her pocket.

The prick of Jack's anger still stung, and knowing that she was about to scoop him didn't lessen the hurt. Being the better sneak wasn't such a victory, after all.

She was frightened of being alone with her thoughts during the hour and a half drive, so for diversion, she plugged the adapter for the reel-to-reel recorder into the cigarette lighter and turned it on. Not much to hear, she knew, what with Mama and Saul in Los Angeles, and she was surprised to find she'd caught another phone conversation.

Saul had gone to L.A. early, driving Hawke and some drinking cronies, and had called home just because he'd missed his wife. The conversation explained to Cissy why Hawke and Dave had returned. They *had* used the friend's premiere as a diversion, and had come back to prepare for the wedding. Caro rented a suite in Reno in deference to the superstition about the bride and groom not seeing each other the day before they wed, leaving Hawke alone.

It seemed Cissy hadn't needed Jack's tape after all. But what troubled her now was the obvious love and tenderness between Saul and his wife, qualities sadly lacking in her own life. Feeling a telltale burning in her eyes, she snapped the recorder off and the radio on. A wailing country tune about lost love enveloped her.

Her tears welled over, tempting her to go back for Jack. But he would only send her away, like he'd done the day before and, besides, the wedding began at sunrise.

The idea came like a lightning bolt from nowhere. True it was too late to get Jack, but she could continue on to Two Moon Bridge, record the ceremony, run her video, snap her photos. Then she'd take the whole lot back to Jack and drop it at his feet. She had no illusions that her gesture would win him back, but at least he'd know she hadn't been using him.

By the time she passed the entrance to the Rockin' Hawke and headed on to Two Moon Bridge, she felt dizzy with relief.

The falling moon was still casting silvery rays when Cissy hid the Jeep in a stand of pine trees and its light eliminated the need for a flashlight that would increase her risk of being caught. She carried her equipment down a rocky trail to a mesa overlooking the wedding site, and by the time she'd set up the last of the tripods behind a stone alcove that kept them from being viewed from the path, the sky was lightening.

She read somewhere that Native Americans called this first waning of the star-studded night "little light," and Cissy now gazed through it to the vista below. Two Moon Bridge was every bit as spectacular as the map lady had promised. The edges of the circles seemed to glow as the cameoed "little light" shone through. Behind her, a narrow stream babbled over rocks and joined with frogs and crickets in a night song. As the stream approached the bridge, it fell sharply, forming a waterfall that terminated in a foaming pool behind the arch.

Down there, parked a distance to the right, were several darkened motor homes, which Cissy assumed were front-runners for the wedding party. As she watched, someone turned on a light.

Cissy breathed in an appreciative breath, then hooked the reel-to-reel to its battery pack and activated it, hoping the bugs she'd put in the saddles weren't dislodged during the ride out. If her luck held, she'd pick up some electrifying quotes. With everything now in readiness, she settled on a rock and opened up a doughnut-shop bag.

She'd just washed down a bite of doughnut when she heard the sound. Feet crunching on gravel! Faraday had a security team scouring the area, she concluded. Oh, Lord, she'd been afraid of that.

Scared to move, she held her paper cup midair and listened. The crunching stopped. She wanted to breathe a sigh of relief, but it was too soon, someone might hear.

"Cissy?" came a whispered voice. She nearly flew off her perch.

"Cissy!" Louder this time. She tiptoed forward and saw Jack searching every nook and cranny of the crude path that led to her hiding place.

"Shh." She rushed out and dragged him aside. "Faraday has men out here. They'll hear."

Jack shook his head. "There's no one else. Just us."

"You scared the hell out of me!" she scolded, staring up at him. Jack merely smiled. Gone was the sour expression of the previous day.

"How did you find me?"

"A hint—never rent a red car to do undercover work. I followed you from the motel."

Cissy's heart sank. "To scoop me on the story?"

"No. I came to give it to you."

"Give! Give me? It's already mine!" With a toss of her curls, she slapped her hands on her hips. "I'm going to give it to *you*. At least I was." She stepped closer. "You are the most arrogant, interfering man I have—"

"Shut up, Cissy." Jack bent to kiss her.

She was going to fight, really she was, but somehow it didn't seem polite, not after all they'd been through. So, instead, she sighed, and tasted him. Better than any old doughnut and coffee, that was for sure.

When he sighed in return, she thought she heard relief in the sound. After the kiss ended, she leaned against him and listened to the reassuring sound of his heart.

"I love you, Cissy." He breathed the words into her hair. "I want to marry you, if you'll have me."

"M-marry me?" Startled, she pulled back. "Just a few hours ago you told me to get out of your room. What caused this change of heart?"

"I got a call from JoJo," he said. "It explained a lot."

"Yeah, which made me mad as hell. Aren't you mad?"

"How could I be? He brought us together didn't he?" He pulled her close again. "Now, about my question...?"

Just then a flock of birds took flight. Earthbound creatures scurried in the underbrush. Cissy smiled. "Come on, Jack. I think our story is arriving."

They went to the edge of the mesa to find the rising sun painting the landscape in roses and golds. A sienna cloud in the distance signaled of approaching riders.

Cissy turned on her video camera, then began adjusting her thirty-five millimeter. "Where's your equipment, Jack?"

Grinning, he pulled a hand-held camera with a long lens from beneath his jacket. "Rookies always overprepare."

But Cissy was too busy focusing to pay much attention.

Wearing a western tuxedo of sequin-studded hot pink, Hawke sat astride one of the palominos, leading the second one behind him. It carried no rider. Cissy grinned. Looked like Mama had gotten her way, after all.

A cavalcade of cars streamed down the road from the highway, boiling up the dust. People started pouring out of the motor homes. Cissy saw a man in an unadorned hot-pink suit, and only the white band at his neck identified him as the minister.

"Least they didn't hire the Elvis impersonator," Jack quipped.

Cissy smothered her laugh and kept watching. Mama was there, bustling around, attending to details. Dave, who'd ridden in with Hawke on a sedate sorrel, was directing the wedding party to their positions in front of the bridge. Cissy saw several of Hawke's band members and a host of celebrities. She snapped pictures like crazy.

Rows of chairs appeared. People began sitting and soon all was quiet in preparation for the bride's appearance.

Mama tied the second palomino to one of the motor homes, disappeared inside and came out a few seconds later with Caro. Cissy gritted her teeth enviously as she took in the snowy wedding dress. Actually it was a pant dress, which Cissy soon saw when Caro climbed astride the horse. But it glittered from shoulder to white boot, and a large white Stetson heaped with billowing chiffon graced the model's head.

Caro paused after mounting and rode slowly toward the temporary altar. Too slowly, Cissy thought.

"Something's going on," she whispered, her eyes still glued to her camera. With her peripheral vision, she saw Jack nod.

Instead of riding down the aisle between the chairs

as expected, Caro directed her palomino toward the far side.

"What is she doing?" Jack murmured.

Cissy didn't know, but she abandoned the camera and ran to the recorder to turn up the volume and heard a rush of voices asking the same question.

By the time Cissy returned to the ridge, Caro had stopped her horse beside the front row and was staring down it.

"I can't do this, Dave," she said, tears in her voice.

"Do what?" came Hawke's gravel voice.

Through her lens, Cissy saw Dave's astonished face, which was mirrored by the other faces around him. He stood up and began walking toward Caro.

She dismounted. They both began running. When Caro reached Dave, he circled her waist and spun her around. Her words were lost in the roar of the spectators.

But Hawke's words came through clear. "What the hell?" He jumped off his horse and sprinted toward the couple, rage and confusion covering his rangy features. Their audience quieted, suddenly all ears.

Hawke tore Caro from Dave's arms. "Get your fanny back on that horse," he ordered. "We got a wedding to get through."

Dave stepped up and removed Hawke's hand from Caro's wrist. "Don't you get it? She's not marrying you, man."

"That's ridiculous!"

"No, Hawke, it isn't." Caro's reedy voice held none of the sultry sophistication Cissy heard that day on the patio. "I can't go through with this. I'm in love with Dave."

"We almost got married in Reno Saturday night," Dave said. "But Caro couldn't stand to hurt you."

Cissy glanced over at Jack and raised a pregnant eyebrow. Hurt Hawke? He'd bury his sorrows in the arms of the next willing woman. Jack's return grimace told her he thought the same thing.

"Is that true?" Hawke sounded truly astonished.

"So marry Dave then, Caro," one of the spectators shouted. "We came a long way for this wedding. Give us one."

"Yes! Yes! Yes! Yes!" came echoing cries. The group broke into a chant. "Wed-ding! Wed-ding! Wed-ding!"

Hawke divided his glare between Dave, Caro and his guests. "So who's your husband of choice?" he asked Caro.

"We do have a license," she said sweetly, moving closer to Dave. "Did you bring it?"

Dave patted his pocket and looked at Hawke. "You suppose I could get you to lend me that suit, man?"

Hawke grunted. "You're nuts, Caro, you know that? You could have had the Hawke." He turned then, and went back to the palomino. As he rode away, he called back, "I hope you both rot in hell."

"You know," Jack said as the new murmur from the crowd erased all fears of being overheard. "I always thought there was something phony about Caro's come-ons. Do you think she was trying to provoke Hawke into breaking it off?"

"Could be."

Then, unable to hold it any longer, Cissy broke into a whoop of laughter. A second later Jack joined her. Holding on to one another, they laughed, then laughed again and barely recovered in time to shoot pictures of the wedding.

When the last shot had been taken, Cissy gave Jack a thoughtful look. ''If you ask me, Jack, this is a story for *Movers & Shakers.*''

Jack had been wearing an eternal smile since the sudden twist in the wedding, but now it faded. ''No, Cissy. This is your story. I meant what I said.''

''Doesn't your magazine have room for a rookie?'' Cissy felt suddenly shy. ''If I remember right, you asked me to be your wife.''

''So now she gets around to accepting.'' Jack swept her into his arms and planted a kiss on her nose. ''You bet, Tinker Bell. We've plenty of room for a rookie.''

''Good. But one more thing.'' She stood on tiptoe. ''Don't call me that anymore.''

Then she kissed the man she loved.

* * * * *

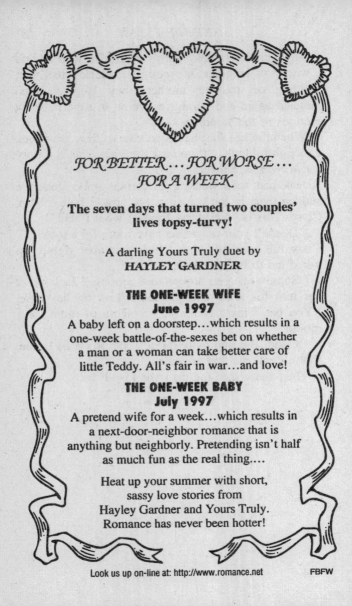

FOR BETTER... FOR WORSE... FOR A WEEK

**The seven days that turned two couples'
lives topsy-turvy!**

A darling Yours Truly duet by
HAYLEY GARDNER

THE ONE-WEEK WIFE
June 1997

A baby left on a doorstep...which results in a
one-week battle-of-the-sexes bet on whether
a man or a woman can take better care of
little Teddy. All's fair in war...and love!

THE ONE-WEEK BABY
July 1997

A pretend wife for a week...which results in
a next-door-neighbor romance that is
anything but neighborly. Pretending isn't half
as much fun as the real thing....

Heat up your summer with short,
sassy love stories from
Hayley Gardner and Yours Truly.
Romance has never been hotter!

FBFW

And the Winner Is...
You!

...when you pick up these great titles
from our new promotion at your
favorite retail outlet this June!

Diana Palmer
The Case of the Mesmerizing Boss

Betty Neels
The Convenient Wife

Annette Broadrick
Irresistible

Emma Darcy
A Wedding to Remember

Rachel Lee
Lost Warriors

Marie Ferrarella
Father Goose

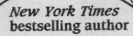

IN CELEBRATION OF MOTHER'S DAY, JOIN
SILHOUETTE THIS MAY AS WE BRING YOU

a funny thing

HAPPENED ON THE WAY TO THE

DELIVERY ROOM

THESE THREE STORIES, CELEBRATING THE
LIGHTER SIDE OF MOTHERHOOD, ARE
WRITTEN BY YOUR FAVORITE AUTHORS:

KASEY MICHAELS
KATHLEEN EAGLE
EMILIE RICHARDS

When three couples make the trip to the delivery
room, they get more than their own bundles of
joy…they get the promise of love!

Available this May,
wherever Silhouette books are sold.

This summer, the legend
continues in Jacobsville

Diana Palmer

A LONG, TALL
TEXAN SUMMER

Three **BRAND-NEW** short stories

This summer, Silhouette brings readers a special
collection for Diana Palmer's LONG, TALL TEXANS
fans. Diana has rounded up three **BRAND-NEW**
stories of love Texas-style, all set in Jacobsville,
Texas. Featuring the men you've grown to love from
this wonderful town, this collection is a must-have
for all fans!

*They grow 'em tall in the saddle in Texas—and
they've got love and marriage on their minds!*

Don't miss this collection of original Long, Tall Texans
stories...available in June at your favorite retail outlet.

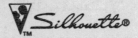